FLEETING CHILLS

WEIRD, CREEPY, SHORT & SCARY HORROR STORIES

JOSEPH C. GIOCONDA,
AUTHOR & EDITOR

ISBN: 978-1-7372860-7-3 (Paperback)
ASIN: B09BBDFWWF (eBook)

Library of Congress Cataloguing-in-Publication Data

Front cover image by selfpubbookcovers.com/JohnBellArt

All illustrations licensed from iStockPhoto and Shutterstock except *Mausoleum* by Demonrat

First digital edition September 2021

Published by Newtown IP Holdings LLC
301 South State Street, Suite 102S
Newtown PA 18940

"Hell is empty, and all the devils are here."

-William Shakespeare, the Tempest

CONTENTS

ACKNOWLEDGEMENTS

I want to thank the fellow writers and filmmakers who have influenced the way we experience horror: Poe, King, Koontz, Lovecraft, Barker, Shelley, Stoker, Serling, Bradbury, Romero, Craven, and many more. We fellow horror writers labor in their towering shadows.

And, as always, I want to thank another fellow author, my wife Alison, for keeping an eye on our children while I disappeared at night to complete this book.

WARNING

Fleeting Chills contains descriptions of murder and self-injury as well as other material that some readers may consider triggering. Reader discretion is advised.

The authors and editor did not include such material gratuitously, but rather to reflect true horror.

AUTHOR'S & EDITOR'S NOTE

Usually, I put my author's note at the end of my books. But in this case, I think a little context up front is necessary.

We all find ourselves musing over weird ideas and little stories in our heads, don't we? They may pop into our minds after scanning a headline in the news, reading a memorable Reddit post, overhearing someone else's conversation, or ripped from a genuine nightmare that wakes us up in a sweat. Sometimes, a single word may trigger the muse.

In many of these cases, our brainchildren don't have much of a beginning, a middle, or an end. Characters don't develop narrative arcs that deserve full treatment in a book. Nonetheless, terrifying flights of fancy spring from the deep subconscious, are often thought-provoking and demand to be shared, no matter how horrifying.

For authors, short stories can be more difficult to write than an entire novel. When writing a book, an author can leisurely spend time setting the scene, developing characters (including minor ones), and exploring subplots. In a good short story, every word should count. For that reason, aspiring writers are instructed to spend a fair amount of time honing the craft of penning short stories before moving on to full-length novels. Despite their difficulty level, shorter narratives are fun to write, and many successful novelists find time to write some good ones.

I have selectively curated several stories written by aspiring writers in the United States, the United Kingdom, and other countries. Their styles and subjects are as diverse as their voices. I have only lightly edited them to retain their voice and have left the British spelling when appropriate. I am honored to publish their work alongside mine, and I am confident that every one of these authors will achieve great things.

Some of the tales in this book could fairly be called "bite-sized" or "ultra-short" stories. Most traditional horror-genre short stories are about 1,500 words or more. Certainly, the best of all time by Edgar Allan Poe came in under 2,100 words. O Henry's *Gift of the Magi* was around the same length. My own short stories average around 1,500, but some are as short as a few hundred words. The other authors' stories included range in length, as well, but some come closer to the traditional 2,500 words.

I believe that a terrifying concept can theoretically be communicated in two sentences. They say brevity is the soul of wit. In some ways, it is also the soul of horror. Our own warped imaginations fill in the gaps. Plus, our attention spans have shortened since Poe's time thanks to movies, video games, and the introduction of flash fiction and "creepypastas," brief horror-themed stories circulating on the Internet.

For readers, short stories are a good deal. Because they are each independent plots that don't require continuity for more than one chapter, they don't require much time, effort, or concentration to read or remember. In fact, when I was younger, I distinctly recall short horror stories making a stronger impression on me than longer ones. For example, television shows like *Tales from the Darkside*, the vignettes in *Creepshow*, and books that contained anthologies of short stories burned concepts into my mind for life. Certainly, Rod Serling's *Twilight Zone* and Ray Bradbury's shorter works are also masterpieces, despite their length.

The format of the stories included in this book varies. In some cases, they are written from the first-person's point of view, the protagonist having experienced the events firsthand. In other contexts, they are written in the traditional third-person narrative prose. The styles seemed to fit the stories; there is no rhyme or reason to the formatting. I personally find that the "confession" style where a narrator describes events happening to them is among the most compelling for horror-themed short stories. Such was the case in Poe's *The Telltale Heart.*

In any event, a typical reader can easily read two or three stories in a day. Maybe (hopefully!) you will find yourself unable to put this book down and can't help but read them all in one sitting. They are not included in any order. I hope that you find at least a few to be horrific, and I hope they stick in your subconscious long after you put this book down and give you chills.

As for subject matter, "horror" is a subjective concept that changes from time to time, according to the milieu. If you look at the concept from decades past, it often mirrored the socioeconomic struggles of the day. As religiosity waned in the modern world, much of horror has drifted away from tales of supernatural devils toward equally frightening stories of mental illness, psychosis, serial killers, evil scientists, and paranormal events. These stories contain a variety of these themes.

One final and very important note: Many of these stories are based on true accounts that I can personally verify. But I won't tell you which ones. Enjoy them all.

1

CONVERTIBLE

By Joseph C. Gioconda

I died that Monday. Well, not exactly. It turns out we can't die. We just switch into a different, parallel timeline and continue living, although that alternative universe might be a little different. It's called quantum immortality.

Let me try to explain.

It was a humid summer morning, July 15, 2013, to be exact. I had recently bought a fire red 2002 convertible Thunderbird, so I was excited to drive it with the canvas top down and the music up, even though it was only 8:15 a.m. I kept my old beat-up Jeep and would put the convertible in the garage during the rough winters in the Midwest.

It had rained and been crappy all weekend, so I had used the Jeep, but the temperature this morning had already hit eighty degrees. It was going to be a nice hot day, even if I had to spend most of it indoors at my office. I backed the convertible out of the garage and down my driveway.

I was on my way to work, where I was an engineer of sorts. I tediously fixed the machines that made medicinal tablets at a medium-size pharmaceutical company called Concourse Pharmaceuticals, located about twelve miles from my home. While others might find it boring, I loved my job; it was fun, stable with great benefits, and the pay wasn't too bad. I also worked with some awesome people like my boss Harry and my friend Jack. Jack was a single guy and a riot. As a married man, I loved hearing the stories of his weekend exploits.

My wife Nancy was not thrilled with my latest car purchase or my job. We'd been having some tough times in our marriage. Most couples fight about money. Others argue about sex or the kids. We argued about politics.

Nancy was a feminist flamethrower who had graduated from Berkeley and went to work at several non-profits after college. She believed the public interest mattered most. I, on the other hand, had been raised as a conservative Republican, just like my brother Glenn and sister Maggie. Thanksgiving dinners would always involve a big family fight, as Maggie and my wife would rail against each other about feminist politics. Glenn and I would laugh and watch them go at it; it was great fun, even if our collective blood pressure would go up during the arguments. I never thought when I married her that Nancy and my family and I would be going at each other's throats about politics so much, but there we were. At least until that Monday.

I turned the round knob on the radio to blast a new song that I liked. I approached the intersection and got ready to take a left-hand turn. This was a notoriously dangerous spot on any given day, and there had been many accidents there. I took this same route daily: sun, rain, or snow. I had always thought it was hard to see if the intersection was clear from the right. The left turn was particularly hazardous, and trucks often barreled through it. I had a few close calls with them over the years.

That Monday, I was running a little late as I toyed with the radio. I had an important meeting at nine with Harry that we'd been planning for carefully over several weeks, and a stupid delay getting showered and dressed at the last minute put all that in jeopardy.

Consequently, I approached the intersection distracted and in a hurry. I rolled through the stop sign a little too far and quickly glanced to the right. I believed that I saw nothing was approaching, so I made the left turn as usual. As I crossed the intersection, I glanced right once more, and this time, I saw an eighteen-wheeler heading straight for me at what could only have been seventy miles per hour. We saw each other. I saw the look in the truck driver's eyes because we really were that close for an instant. He grimaced and braked hard. But he knew what was happening next. A deadly collision was inevitable. There was no way on this earth that it could have been avoided at that speed. We both braced for the fatal impact.

The rest of the drive to my office was too fuzzy to remember. I distinctly remember that the song I was listening to wasn't playing any longer, even though I knew it had just started.

Another odd thing was that I was no longer in my convertible. I was sitting in my Jeep. But I had no recollection of going back home and switching cars. Could I have gotten a concussion from an accident and ended up driving home, getting my Jeep, and going to work? Maybe, but I had no recollection of doing that, and where was my convertible?

When I pulled up to work, I was sweating. Not just from the heat and humidity but from stress. And something else was odd—my assigned parking spot at work, which had my favorite number painted in yellow on the ground (#49), was gone. There were no numbered spots at all.

And how could they paint the parking lot over the weekend and cover up all the numbers? There didn't seem to be paint over the numbers on the ground; it was like the numbers were never there. I reminded myself to ask the staff when I could have my lucky spot number re-painted.

I walked inside my office atrium to sign in and show my identification card. The sign said "Techbiotics." I didn't recognize the receptionist. I pulled out my wallet to show my card to her, and it said "Techbiotics" on it. Impossible. Just then, Jack walked out of the doorway.

"Hey, man, did you drive the convertible to work today?"

"Um, yeah," I stammered. "Well, no. I thought I did. I drove the Jeep. I'm a little confused. Jack, what's with the company name?"

"What about it?"

"Well, what happened to Concourse?"

"What?" he asked, bemused. "What the hell is Concourse?"

"Uh, just where we worked for the last two years, moron," I said.

Jack laughed, "Are you day drinking? Don't tell Sandy or Mike; you'll get canned."

"Sandy? Mike?" I asked, becoming even more confused. "Who are they?"

"Sandy, the CEO? Mike, your boss?" Jack was starting to look at me strangely. "Come on; you clearly need some stronger coffee than usual."

"I can't," I said. "I don't have time. I have a meeting at 9 with Harry."

"Who's Harry?"

"Um, my boss?" I said.

"You mean Mike?"

"Wait, Harry got canned? That's not possible; he e-mailed me just this weekend to confirm. Look…" I pulled out my iPhone and scrolled through my e-mails. "Wait, I must have deleted it. Look, I don't know what's going on, but maybe I do need some coffee before this meeting, *pronto*."

We quickly walked over to the Starbucks coffee shop next door. I ordered my usual double espresso.

"Hitting the caffeine hard today, my man? Good move," Jack commented. "What's going on with you? Are you ok?"

"Dude, I get super strong coffee every morning; what are you talking about?"

Jack just shrugged. "I thought you only drank decaf."

The remainder of my morning was relatively uneventful, except that all my stationery and computers now said "Techbiotics" instead of "Concourse." I couldn't figure out for the life of me how they could have possibly changed out all the materials over the weekend. My new boss "Mike" never showed up to the meeting, and neither did Harry. Harry's office was totally empty, his name tag missing from the desk and door.

They must have fired him in a hurry because it was a clutter of files and folders on Friday. Even his Ficus tree was gone.

My mind kept wandering back to the non-accident that morning. Could I have hit my head somehow and gotten a concussion or amnesia or something? I intended to see a doctor if I continued to feel this weird. Something was seriously wrong. I felt fundamentally different.

When I walked in the front door to my house that afternoon, everything was just… off. First, Nancy was dressed in a sexy outfit. She came over and kissed me full on the lips.

"How's my hubby doing today? Why didn't you take the convertible to work? It's still in the garage with the car cover on it. God, I love that thing. I'm jealous on days like today."

But my wife hated that car. Yet, she didn't sound like she was being her usual sarcastic self about it.

"No, I thought I did, but I guess I took the Jeep. I had to find a new parking spot at work. What's going on?"

"Nothing, I was just watching that awful Obama on the news."

"What?" I laughed, "Obama? Like your favorite guy?"

She looked at me, "Favorite? God, he is so awful."

I was baffled and figured she must be joking.

"Nancy, I had something really strange happen today. Remember how my company was called Concourse?" I asked her.

"Um, no. When was that? You've worked at Techbiotics for years now. You hate it, remember?"

"No, I don't. I love Concourse. What the hell are you talking about?"

Nancy gazed at me quizzically. "Look!"

She handed me a framed photograph of me and my co-workers skydiving at a company retreat. Sure enough, we were holding a banner that said "Techbiotics Rocks!"

"You always told me that you hated it, but I supported you staying there."

I sat down abruptly. "Nancy," I said, "I am really confused. I have a *very* strange story to tell you."

She sat down, looking concerned and nervous. "Did you get fired?"

"No," I said. I proceeded to tell her about the near truck accident and my missing memories and confusing day.

She was concerned and put her hand on my arm. "Sweety, that's awful; I'm just glad you are ok."

"But I'm not ok," I said. "Everything is wrong."

"That happens sometimes, especially with heat stroke; maybe you're just dehydrated," she said, abruptly changing the subject. "By the way, are you inviting your brother Glenn to the summer house in August?"

"Yeah, I was going to," I said.

"Great, we always have such a great time," she said.

"Are you being sarcastic?"

"No, why?" she asked.

"Never mind," I said. "I'll probably invite Maggie too, as long as you don't get into another big argument with her like last Thanksgiving."

"Maggie?" Nancy asked, confused.

"Um, my sister?" I laughed.

"Your sister?" Nancy stared at me.

"Yes, *my sister* Maggie," I emphasized.

Nancy became silent for a moment.

"Honey, you know your sister died when you were twelve."

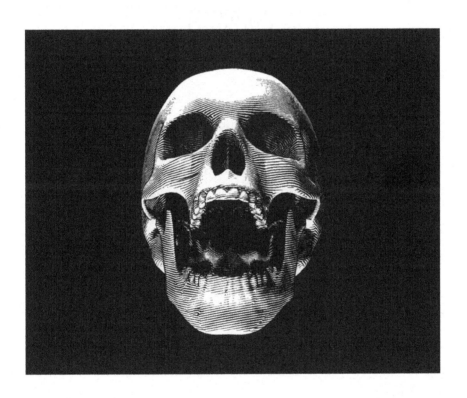

TEETH

By Joseph C. Gioconda

"**W**here'd you say you got this skull?"

The owner of the antique shop stretched a blue latex glove over the fingers of his right hand. He wiped his thin graying hair over his balding forehead and adjusted his thick eyeglasses. The dealer specialized in macabre items and had developed a large inventory and robust following of collectors. Most of the items consisted of Victorian mourning items, urns containing cremated remains, and curious funerary objects.

"eBay. This was back in the nineties when they still let us buy and sell human body parts online." The tall, muscular man leaned on the glass counter. "Med school students bought them for anatomy projects or whatever."

"Right," the shop owner said, gingerly picking up the human cranium to examine it. "Are you a doctor or something?"

"No," the tall man said. "I had a fleeting interest in those kinds of dark things back then."

The shop owner looked up at the man and back to the skull he now held in his hand. The lower jaw was unattached and stayed in the box.

"Upper teeth look really good," he said, holding the skull up to the light. "Mandible's intact, too."

"Yeah, it's a great specimen."

"How much did you pay for it?" the shop owner asked him.

"Let me look…," the tall man pulled a double-folded piece of paper out of the brown tattered cardboard box. "Looks like I paid eight hundred fifty bucks back in ninety-nine."

"Can I see that printout?"

"No, I'd rather not." The man shoved it into his front jeans pocket.

"Why is that?"

"I just like to keep my eBay screenname and details private, sorry."

"Well, from what I can tell, and I'm certainly no expert, this looks like it might be a young woman's skull."

"Good eye," the tall man said. "That's what it said in the listing."

"Probably in her mid-twenties based on the size of the eye sockets," said the dealer. "It's been bleached," he continued, turning it around to look at the back of the head.

"What do you mean?"

"Whenever bones are preserved for any kind of medical use, the taxidermist manually strips off the raw flesh, whatever meat and skin is hanging off. They scrape out the eyeballs and try to remove the brain material that's stuck in there. Then, they let the bone sit in acid for a while. Sometimes a few days to a week. That gets the rest of the flesh to putrefy to liquid. After that, bone is usually yellow. To get it whiter, they let it sit in bleach for a while. It's just aesthetic. Collectors like to display white bones, not yellow."

"I see," the man said.

"Ups the value a bit, but it makes it a little harder to visually date. I can't tell how old this one is. It must be modern because the back teeth have fillings in them, see?"

The dealer used his pinky finger to point at the top molars, which had silver and ceramic treatments still compressed inside.

"Could someone figure out how old it is by carbon dating the bone or whatever they call it? Look at dental records?"

"Sure, but that's pretty expensive," said the dealer. "Police wouldn't typically do that with some random modern skull bought off eBay. Most are just from India."

"India? Why is that?" the man asked.

"Skeleton farms there."

"What?"

"International treaty from way back. All legal human skeletons must come from India. But anyway, I doubt this one is from there."

"Why's that?" the man asked.

"The structure of the skull doesn't look Indian, and, like I said, the fillings are modern. Ceramic and mercury fillings aren't typical in India. At least among the castes whose bones get exported. No, I'm guessing this girl was American. Maybe South American, Brazilian. Hard to say. The real oddity is that her noggin' ended up being sold on eBay. Where did this shipment come from?"

"Original box had no return address. I don't remember the post office date or location stamp. I threw it out years ago. Anyway, do we have a deal or not?"

"What do you want for her?"

"Just what I paid. Eight fifty."

"No profit?"

"No, I just want to be rid of it."

"Why is that?"

"My new girlfriend doesn't like it hanging around the apartment. I used to keep it in a glass case on my Xbox. She thought that was too creepy, so about two years ago, I put it in a storage locker. But I was afraid the heat might do damage, and I could use the extra cash to buy an engagement ring for her."

"I see."

"So, do we have a deal?"

"Yeah, that price seems fair."

The dealer carefully placed the skull back in the box on the newspapers. "I'll write up a receipt."

"No, that's ok. I prefer to just take the cash."

"Well, I have to put something in the file. It's the law. We're talking about a human head here."

"Sure, name's John."

"Ok, John. Last name?"

"Jones."

"John Jones?" The dealer looked up at the man skeptically.

"Right."

"Ok, John Jones. Are large bills ok?" The antique dealer opened the cash register and peeled out eight one-hundred-dollar bills and a fifty.

"Yes, perfect." He put the money in his wallet. "So let me ask you this… what are you going to do with it?"

"I have a roster of collectors. Frankly, I'll tag it for a thousand and negotiate. Probably only make a small profit on it."

"What do your buyers do with them? Light them up on Halloween or something?" the man asked.

"Well, some do. The woman I have in mind to buy this one actually does psychic readings on them."

"What do you mean?"

"She's a psychic or medium, or whatever. Or she thinks she is anyway. She'll do a séance or something, to try to see if there are any spirit attachments."

"Why?"

"I guess she wants to try to see whose head it was, I don't really know. Maybe get it to talk. She records voices on a digital recorder. It's called EVP's, electronic voice phenomena. Pretty creepy stuff, actually."

"Does it ever work?" the man asked.

"Does what work?"

"Does she ever really uncover who the skull had belonged to?"

"She must think so. She has a lot of them. I think one time, she solved a cold case that way. Voice gave her the name of the killer, I think."

"Can I ask a favor?" the man asked.

"What is it?" the dealer asked him curiously.

"Here's my cell number." He scribbled a telephone number with a Texas area code on a scrap of paper. "If you hear back from her, and if she comes up with a theory of whose skull it was, can you tell me?"

"Interested in what she finds out?"

"You could say that. And please ask her not to broadcast it publicly before you tell me."

"Why's that?"

"Just ask her, please, ok?"

"Um, sure," said the dealer.

"One last thing, let me take back the cardboard box it's in."

"Oh, I was going to use that for storage until my collector comes in to pick it up."

"Don't you have another box?"

"Um, maybe, let me look," the dealer looked around for a sturdier box. He took the skull out and placed it in a wooden one. "There you go. You can have it back."

The man took back the cardboard box and pulled out the old newspapers.

"Here, you can actually throw out my old one; I just wanted the padding out of it."

The dealer didn't notice that the skull's teeth looked a lot like the smiling girl's photos in the crumpled-up newspapers in the man's hand.

JUMP

By Grace Elizabeth

His therapist told him to jump at every opportunity.

Vince had been staring at the wall for hours. The white of the wall merged with the red of the blood that covered the foot of his bed.

His arms ached but didn't sting; the dull ache which reverberated down his limbs was simply in his mind—it no longer hurt. The sensation of cutting himself used to be something he would wince at, flinch as the knife pierced his skin, but now he felt nothing. And as he drew the knife back up his arm, watching the small beads of blood form like fine wine, he couldn't help but laugh.

Who was he becoming?

He stared at the smashed glass on the floor; the voices had told him to do it. They were antagonising, and he could only ignore them for so long; every scream he heard, every giggle which echoed throughout his mind was a reminder that he wasn't normal. He wasn't like everyone else, and he never would be again.

The voices dominated him completely, engulfed his personality, his desires, his deepest thoughts… and there wasn't a single thing he could do about it. He just had to sit there and wait for it to pass.

Every time he picked up the knife and put the blade to his skin, it felt like a release, every time he made a new incision, he felt as if he was silencing the voices just for a moment. For a few blissful seconds, it was silent. He heard nothing but the sound of his own breathing. And in those rare moments, he focused on the beating of his heart, the feeling of blood pumping through his frail veins, reminding himself that he was okay.

Of course, none of it was true; these pointless affirmations he gave himself were just to keep him away from the edge, to keep him as far from the edge of suicide as possible. But he couldn't help but admit that every time he looked at a knife or a blade or a fork or a sharp surface, he fantasised about plunging it into himself, about ending his life. He had always thought people cowards for committing suicide until he was sixteen—that was when he first attempted it.

He remembered holding the bottle of pills, the sound of them rattling against the sides of the bottle as his hands, trembling uncontrollably, beckoned him to take them, to swallow every morsel of the contents. He ached to feel the cold of the water force them down his throat, feel it land in his stomach, and the voices praise him—say things like "good" and "well done." Their praise was all that mattered to him; it was everything he strived for—he had lost his family, lost his job, lost himself—this was all he had left.

He had tried to speak to someone about it; countless therapists and counsellors had tried to help him. Each one had given him the same useless advice. Over and over, he would be given the same checklist.

1. Go for a walk, get some fresh air.
2. Drink some tea, it soothes the soul.
3. Write it all down in a journal.

But you see, he had no need to write it all down in a book that would be more permanent than his life, that would be more consistent than the things echoing through his head. He had no need to go for a walk. If he did, he might just end up walking off the edge of a cliff or over the top of a bridge. He had no need to drink tea when he could drink bourbon or whiskey. Both burnt his throat; both soothed his soul—but this was so much easier to handle when he was blacked out on the floor of his bathroom in a pool of his own blood.

Nobody would understand; the voices told him that every day—repeated that they were there for him, laughed and mocked him as he broke down on the floor, his tears were the only part of him that felt human anymore. He felt like he had leaked every ounce of blood from his body, every morsel of happiness had disintegrated when these voices took over, when these voices decided it was their life, not his.

Vince knew that he had committed some awful crimes in his life-time; he had hurt people purely because the voices which rattled in his head had begged him to. They never found the body of the first person he murdered, and they never would. He had hidden him too well... the voices had told him how to do it; they had guided him through one of the most difficult moments of his life. As horrific as they were, they comforted him more than they scared him.

He had first seen the jogger while out on a walk. His therapist had told him that he should focus more on the nature around him, and so he did. He went walking in a forest, which was the most tranquil place he had ever seen. It was full of woodland creatures and the most beautiful plants.

Upon the rise of the sun, the forest was covered in a blanket of white. It had a majestic aura that begged the lost souls of those who wandered the icy woods to stop—just for a moment—and embrace the feeling of tranquility. The frozen lake met the winter sun with such grace as if the two of them were so enchanted by the serenity of the cool winter day that they barely noticed the chilling air.

The river appeared still, yet she flowed under the thinnest of ice, awaiting the brutally gentle touch of the sun. Though the air bared only the coldness and the ground was frozen over, they glittered with the gift of each individual shining ray. It was almost as if a higher power ensured there would be hope even on the deepest and most dreary of days, asking us to see the sparks that remain even when the world around us was frozen. It was bitterly cold, but somehow the rays of the sun warmed the cheeks of those who entered the forest—it was an enchanting combination. Every blade of grass and twig was frozen upwards like stubborn ice crystals determined not to break. A harsh, freezing fog lingered throughout the trees and over the lakes—daring anybody who trespassed on such beauty to try and vandalise it. The only sounds that could be heard were the gentle tweets of various birds preparing for easier times when they wouldn't have to flee their nests. Should you venture far enough into the woods, far enough that the dense canopy of trees blocked the radiant sun out, you might be lucky enough to come across a wild deer, gnawing away at a stray patch of grass or trying to get to a small hole in the ice. It was the type of place you would feel completely and utterly safe, where nothing could harm you; there was no anger or malice in the forest, just captivating beauty and frivolous happiness. Small shrubs and delicate flowers lay flat on the ground, covered in a duvet of crystal white snow, completely concealed by the power of the winter. However cold the harsh winter became, in the forest, you could rest assured that no matter what you felt, the memories you had experienced in your life would flood back full force. The good memories you held would seem extraordinary, and the rather terrible ones wouldn't seem so bad at all. The forest seemed magical, a truly captivating and enchanting haven.

He looked around, and that was when he saw him. That was when the voices started whispering to him, telling him to hurt the jogger for what he had done to the world. What he did was simple; he wasn't a big man.

He simply gripped the back of his head and slammed it into the tree until he fell limp in his arms. Just to make sure he would never hurt another person again, he did something that would ensure his death.

He dumped the lifeless corpse into his car and began to drive. He couldn't tell if the sound that filled his car was the sound of the jogger choking or the voices in his head, and he didn't care. He did what he had to do; he had done the right thing, at least that was what the voices kept telling him.

He took the man's body and buried it in a deep hole in the middle of the woods, but that simply wasn't enough—he needed to do more; he needed to cover his tracks. He found a cat roaming the streets that night and petted it slowly. He then took a rock and bashed its head in—smiling as he did as the voices praised him and reassured him that everything would be okay as long as he listened to them.

He filled the hole halfway with dirt and then threw the cat's corpse on top of it; if the sniffer dogs found any trace of the jogger's body, they would simply assume that it was the rotting cat causing such a stench.

He got home and slept like nothing had happened. As the days went by, guilt started to creep into him. It visited him in his dreams and forced him awake screaming, but at the end of the day, the voices were always there to reassure him... at least that was what he thought.

Other voices started to creep in, new voices that he hadn't heard before telling him he was bad for what he did and muttering vile things to him as he tried to fall asleep—the guilt consumed him.

The next month, he went back to the spot and started to dig. He dug holes all over the forest, searching for the dead body just to find him, just to try and bring him back. He finally found him, and he had practically rotted away, mold and moss lined each part of his body, and his skin was discoloured. He hadn't known what rotting flesh smelt like until that night. He threw up over the body and threw it back into the hole from which he had dragged it. He hadn't been the same since that night, the voices had egged him on, and he had started to kill more—they never figured out it was him.

So as Vince stared at himself in the mirror, he didn't see the bright boy that had won the chemistry award last year; he saw a shattered pane of glass. As he slipped on his shoes, he was aware of the way they felt grazing against the skin of his feet. As he pulled his jacket over his arms, he relished the feeling of the cold material on his warm, bleeding arms. And as he stepped out of his door, he could no longer feel the cold; he could only feel the warmth of the crimson red blood cascading down his arms. He stepped from his door to the path and watched the cars go past, the people in them controlling their own thoughts, their own minds, their own desires.

He got to his place, a place his father had taken him when he was young. He sat atop the bridge and stared down at the river, wondering what would happen if he just let himself fall, just let himself hit the water. Would everything be okay again? Would the voices finally leave him alone?

As he threw himself down, he smiled.

After all, his therapist had told him to jump at every opportunity.

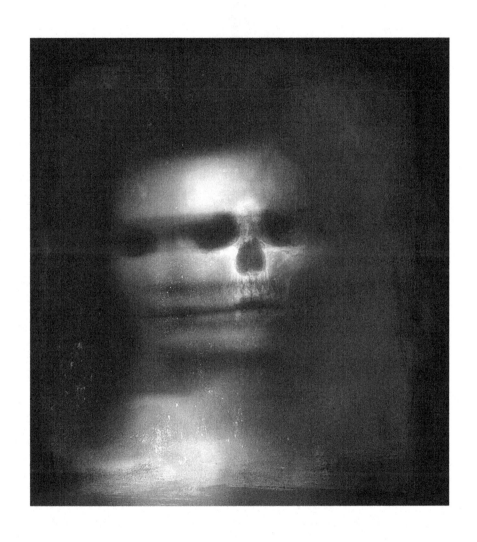

IDENTITY

By Joseph C. Gioconda

"Wait, are you telling me you are possessed or something?"

"It's complicated, that's all."

"What's complicated?" Hank laughed. "Amanda, you just told me that there's another person living inside you."

"I didn't say it that way."

"You just said there's a girl named Alyssa hiding in your body. What the hell does that mean?"

"Hank, I love you. Please sit down and let me explain."

"God, please do."

He sat down on the bed in Amanda's bedroom. Her apartment was normal. There was nothing to evidence the bizarre story she was relating. They had been dating for six months now, and she had been a perfectly pleasant and stable girlfriend. However, one night, the couple had gotten a little drunk at a party, and Amanda started spilling the beans on her family background—a history that he found difficult to believe.

"Back when I was younger, I was abused. Badly. You know that." She took his hands in hers.

"Yeah, I know you had some terrible things happen; I don't really know the specifics," Hank said. "I don't know if I want to know the full extent of it."

"After I turned nineteen, my parents joined a… cult."

"Like a Satanic cult?" Hank asked.

"No, a religious group, not like devil worship. Just a weird church. Anyway, I was abused by the leader of this group. A lot."

"Jesus," Hank said. "I'm so sorry. I always knew something wasn't right about your family, no offense."

"That's when Alyssa came out."

"What do you mean?"

"Can I show you?" Amanda asked.

"Show me what?"

"Alyssa."

"What?" Hank laughed out loud.

"I'm going to bring her out, ok? You should see it happen if you are going to be my boyfriend."

"Um, ok," Hank said nervously, not having a clue what was about to happen.

"Alright," Amanda said, closing her eyes and starting to wince like she was in pain, squeezing his hands.

"Honey, are you ok?" he asked.

She moved her head and neck in torment. Her eyes twitched, and her mouth drew up in a strange grimace.

"Amanda? I said, are you ok?"

"Hi there, I'm Alyssa," she looked up at him, speaking seductively and hoarsely. "You must be this Hank I keep hearing all about. She told me all about you." Her eyes became black as pools of ink, yet Amanda had bright blue eyes.

Hank laughed. "Great acting Amanda, I must say. You really should be an actress. Did you just put in contact lenses? How did you do that to your eyes?"

"Oh, I'm not Amanda. I told you. I'm Alyssa. And boy, she knows how to pick 'em. You're a good-looking man. I'm going to have some fun with you." She pinched his chin playfully.

"What the hell?" he said. "Ok, this is getting creepy. Knock it off."

"Oh, once I'm out to play, I can't just go away. I need to have some fun first. Maybe, after a while, she can get me to leave again, but not quite yet."

"Ok, this is sick, Amanda. Please stop."

"I told you, this isn't a joke. You wanted to meet me, now you have."

"This is crazy; I can't take it. What's this all about?"

"Amanda couldn't handle what they did to her. That's why I had to come around. See, I can handle it. Weak Amanda couldn't. I'm here to protect her from all the bad things. She is too fragile and prissy to take it. But I can."

Hank just silently stared in disbelief.

"You see, she loves you. I have no idea why. I mean, you're good-looking and all, but I prefer my men a little… stronger. I'm a very different woman than your little Amanda. When I'm out, she doesn't even know what I'm up to. She'll go crawl into a corner inside of us and hide. Meanwhile, I'll go out and do things that she would never do. Evil things. And they'll never catch me."

"Ok, this twisted little game is over. I'm leaving." He stood up to march out the door.

"Fine, fine, I'll go back inside her. Not sure why she brought me out to play anyway. But just know, I'm always around if you need me. And you will. You won't always be satisfied with Amanda. You will need me."

Alyssa closed her eyes and cringed. A single tear welled up in her eye and rolled down her cheek. When she opened them, they were as blue as the sky again.

"Please give me a hug, Hank. Hold me."

"Amanda?"

"Yes, it's me. I needed you to see me switch. So now, you know all of me."

5

ALONE

By Joseph C. Gioconda

"We got an old cot in the waiting room," the mortician told me. "You can sleep in there tonight. It's not very comfortable, but it'll do." Everything smelled of mothballs and formaldehyde.

When my father, brothers, and I had arrived at the funeral home in the rental car, we found a three-room shack in the middle of the desert. The closest town was two miles away and consisted of a one-pump gas station, a post office, and a bank that was open a few hours a week. The closest *bona fide* town with a motel was over twenty miles away. In between there and the funeral home, I didn't see a single house. Not one. In fact, I'm not even sure I saw a passing motorist—just cactus after cactus and an empty highway. We had flown to Phoenix from New York and then made the four-hour drive deep into the desert to this local facility that was handling my Uncle Tim's autopsy and burial.

I hadn't known my uncle that well. He had moved to Arizona when I was a teenager. He was my father's brother, but they weren't all that close either. Tim's wife passed away last year, so we were literally his last surviving family. The now-deceased couple never had any kids, and Eleanor's family was unknown to us. Tim was being buried in the veteran's cemetery up in Flagstaff. My mother wasn't in the best health to travel, so she stayed back home. This was really Dad's responsibility, but we didn't want him to deal with it alone.

"You know we could only get one room at the motel, Mike," my father said. "And it only has two singles. Your older brother is sleeping in a cot too."

"Yeah, but he's sharing a motel room with you guys, not spending the night in a funeral home alone. I'm literally going to be miles away from anyone until morning."

"Oh, stop being a baby. It's not like there'll be anyone to bother you," my father said.

"Then you sleep in here," I said, not joking.

I couldn't believe my family was seriously forcing me to sleep by myself in a funeral parlor occupied by more corpses than living people. I wouldn't have access to transportation, so if I wanted to leave in the middle of the night, I couldn't. I truly would be trapped. Miles and miles of wasteland separated me from other living people.

"I'll close this door to the embalming room," the funeral director said to me, pulling it shut. "It doesn't lock. There are three bodies back there: your uncle's and two others. But don't worry, I'll be back at first light to finish the autopsy and prepare him for burial."

He flipped open the raw cot and handed me an uncomfortable pillow and folded polyester sheets.

"This is all I have for your bedding, but the waiting room couch pillows could do in a pinch."

I tried to look brave. "Sure, I'll be fine. Just point me to the bathroom," I said stoically.

"It's over there." He pointed to a tiny powder room next to the embalming room. "No shower, unfortunately." He turned off the bathroom light.

I hung my black suit on the bathroom door. It dangled like a hanged man in a noose.

"See you in the morning, Mike," my father said, closing the outer door behind him and walking to the rental car with my two brothers.

I was now totally alone in the silent building.

This was back before iPhones or iPads. I had absolutely nothing to do except sit in the waiting room in complete silence. I didn't even have a radio, although I doubt the airwaves reached this spot. The only reading materials were old, dated magazines that I had already flipped through twice.

It was only 9:00 p.m., so I had a good ten hours to go before my family and the funeral director would be back. It was getting dark, and I dreaded the many silent hours ahead of me.

I cursed my family for leaving me here. Right now, my father and brothers were driving toward a comfortable motel where they'd watch cable television, drink cold beer, and maybe even go out and get dinner at a drive-through McDonald's. Instead, I was trapped here in the middle of desolation.

I couldn't believe I didn't stand up for myself. If I had rented my own car, I could have at least figured out some alternative. I might have driven down from the airport in the early morning before the funeral, maybe. Or even slept in the airport parking garage or in a tent on the side of the road. Hell, that would be better than this solitude. The howling coyotes would at least be a sound. Instead, cold silence.

My mind started to drift to what was on the other side of that unlocked door. It was a cheap, hollow one, the kind that a strong push could break through. That was probably why the funeral director never bothered to install a lock on it. What was the point? With an interior door that flimsy, an average size person could push right through the hollow wood. The exterior door didn't look much sturdier, but at least it had a lock. I sat and stared at the interior door.

I thought about my Uncle Tim's body in the refrigerator on the other side of it. It was only about twelve feet away from me—six feet on this side of the door and probably six feet on the other. From the glimpse I caught of it earlier, the embalming room was small. And who did the other two bodies belong to? There couldn't be many people living in this part of the desert, much less three people dying within a few days of each other that would need to be temporarily stored here. That seemed suspicious now that I thought about it. And why did the funeral director even mention other bodies?

I tried to put these jarring thoughts out of my mind. They were only making me more uneasy. I started mulling over my options in the case of an emergency. I hadn't noticed a landline telephone. Then again, what emergency could possibly happen in the next few hours? I just needed to fall asleep. Before I knew it, it would be dawn, and the mortician would be back. I never thought that I would be happy to see one.

I tossed and turned on the uncomfortable old cot that smelled like mothballs. The metal bar in the middle was hurting my back. I thought about switching to the couch, but its covers looked even scratchier and more uncomfortable than the sheets on the cot.

I thought of happier times. When I got back to New York, I would go out for a night of binge drinking. That would be fun. A nightclub, filled with girls and booze and loud music…

Just then, I heard something in the embalming room move.

LIFETIMES

By Joseph C. Gioconda

"**M**ichelle, you don't understand what just happened," Jeremy said, shaking.

"What are you talking about? Sit down." She offered him a seat at their kitchen table.

He sat abruptly, picking up a bottle of water and gulping it.

"Are you ok?" she asked.

"Oliver asked me to take him for a walk down the street. Just the two of us."

"Aw, that's so adorable!"

"I thought so too. For a five-year-old, it's a sweet thing for a kid to ask his father to do. Anyway, we started walking down the street. I held his hand because I'm always worried that he's too close to the edge of the sidewalk, you know. He didn't say much. We went down toward the park a bit, and I asked him, 'what's on your mind, little buddy?'

He said, 'I just wanted to have some time to be alone with you and be peaceful and be out in nature.'"

"He used those words?" His wife stopped drying the dish in her hand and looked at him.

"Yeah. Wait, there's more. I said to him, 'aw, that's really nice, Oliver.'

And he said to me, 'I want you to know that you're one of the best fathers I've ever had.'"

She laughed. "Oh, that's so funny. He really said that?"

"So, then I laughed out loud and said, 'well, that's sweet, honey, but I'm the only father you ever had.'

And he stopped, let go of my hand, looked up at me with an old man's eyes, and said, 'I have had many parents. And many children, across many lifetimes. But you're still one of the best fathers I've ever had.' He then went back to holding my hand and being a typical goofy five-year-old again."

1.

PROPOSAL

By Amy Yun Yu

I t's me who the spirit haunts. Not my house, but me.

Wherever I run, it follows. Its presence has taken away every-thing that I had. My sanity's chipping away, piece by piece.

It wants me, and I've got nowhere to run.

I leaned back in the hard leather seat of Sally's car and looked up at the house in front of me. It was the only house on the street with no sign of life in it. I hated it.

"Come on, Jane, you gotta love what you've got. Most of us can't even dream of owning a house at our age," my best friend commented from the driver's seat.

I rolled my eyes and stepped out. I was the only twenty-year-old on campus who owned a two-story house on Vermilion Street and lived alone. I wasn't allowed to have friends over. That was what my parents demanded when they'd transferred the deed to me.

"I would've loved to live on campus, Sally. With friends," I told her as I climbed up the porch and inserted the key into the lock.

She groaned in frustration.

"You can have them here. Your parents will never know."

I threw her an unimpressed look and stepped inside. She hollered her goodbye from the doorway and then was gone.

Sighing, I switched on the lights to the foyer. They blinked a couple of times before winking out entirely. I cursed this high-maintenance old house under my breath and fished out my phone as I made my way into the living room.

Squelch!

I stopped. I'd stepped into something wet. I didn't remember dropping anything like that on the floor. Sighing, I headed for the light switches, my feet making patterns on the floor.

The moment lights struggled on, I yelped. There was a message written on the floor. With mud... or was it mud? I shuddered as I hesitantly walked towards it. Swallowing, I turned on my phone's torch.

Welcome home, darling!

The words read in the mud with worms crawling in it.

I let out a blood-curdling scream, but there was no one to listen.

My legs became weak and refused to support my weight. I stumbled back a couple of steps before crashing on the cold hard floor of my living room.

I fumbled with my cell phone as I called the police. I don't know what I told them, but I was aware of the silence that followed the call. I stayed there, transfixed on the floor while I waited to hear the familiar police sirens outside.

"We found no sign of breaking and entering. No fingerprints anywhere," Inspector Jake Lowe informed me.

I was still shaking, my arms wrapped around myself, and my cardigan pulled tightly close. I refused to look at the Inspector's face. I knew what he might be thinking.

"Could it be a prank?" he suggested when I refused to say anything.

Without giving him a response, I made my way back to the house. God bless them; the police had cleaned up the entrance to the living room for me. But I still stepped around the dark stains and into the kitchen. With my hands shaking, I fixed myself a cup of coffee and bid the police goodbye. I couldn't think. I refused to think.

That night, I tossed and turned in my bed. My bedroom was colder than usual, and it stank of something decaying. I dragged the laundry basket down to the first floor and checked all my drawers, even under the bed. I found nothing. Giving up, I sprayed half a bottle of air freshener.

The stink refused to leave the next day. It was my day off, and I'd planned so many activities, but the events from the night before and the stink made me frustrated than usual. I was exhausted. At eight in the morning, I dragged myself out of my bed and made my way downstairs, fighting off the ugly taste at the back of my throat.

My eyes found their way to the dark stain on the floor from the night before. When my eyes landed on it, I choked down on a scream.

Good morning, babe.

Once more, the message was written in mud with maggots crawling in it.

I slumped down on the stairs, muffling my cries. What the hell was happening around here?

As I tried to wrap my mind around what I was seeing, I heard the bottom step creak as it usually did under a weight. My cries halted in my throat, and I scrambled back a step.

As I watched, with my eyes wide and heartbeat escalating, muddy footprints formed on the stairs. Heading towards me.

In my terror, I couldn't move. My limbs refused to obey my desperate commands.

When the footprints were close enough, I sprang into action. I turned and rushed towards my bedroom, slammed the door closed, and bolted it. I could still hear the floorboards protesting under the weight of the unseen intruder.

Desperately, I looked for my cell phone. But I'd misplaced it somewhere in my bedspread the night before.

The footsteps stopped just outside my door, and I froze. I waited, my bedroom's clock ticking the seconds as if counting down to something.

Then I heard it—a sigh just outside my door. The temperature dropped, and the windows slammed closed. Their glass rattled in the quiet of the Saturday morning. I turned and rushed towards the bathroom. I closed the door behind me just as the door to my bedroom was kicked open by an invisible force.

I pressed my back against the bathroom door and forced myself to calm down and think.

Sliding down to the cold marble floor, I pulled my knees to my chest. *It is all a dream*, I told myself. Or one of my friends was pulling a prank. A perfect one at that. Such thoughts calmed me down to some extent. Only after I stopped shaking, I opened my eyes and focused on everything around me. *Maybe I should've kept my eyes closed,* I thought, as fear twisted like a hot poker inside me.

On the bathroom floor, someone had drawn arrows in blood. Pointing towards the bathtub. Full of blood mixed in water. And swimming in it were dried flower petals and dead insects.

My vision turned dark, and I blinked everything into focus.

I felt numb as my feet carried me towards the dressing area opposite the tub. My hands reached towards the dress that hung on the wall. A tattered wedding dress covered with dirt and blood. Where the hell had it come from?

On the other side of the closed door, I heard the footsteps again. I turned to find the handles to the door turn. In my dread, I'd forgotten to lock the doors.

My feet refused to hold me up, so I fell. The last thing I remembered was the sound of the door opening and searing pain from where my head collided with the dresser's corner.

I was lying on something soft, and I didn't want to move. The overbearing stink hit me like a ton of bricks, and I bolted upright.

The curtains were pulled closed, but I could tell that it was dark outside. The room was lit up with strange candles. Their sharp gasoline smell made my eyes water. The room was cold, and thick smog hung heavy in the air.

I looked down and shrieked. I was dressed in the battered wedding gown. Blood made stark patterns against the white base, and dead insects decorated it like beads. I pulled the gown away from my body, the old material tearing against my grip.

Ssshhh!! Someone whispered just as the other side of the mattress dipped under the weight. This time, I couldn't even scream. My throat had closed up on me.

This was happening, and it wasn't a dream.

I slid off the bed, crawled, stumbled, and ran towards the door. It was locked. With my hands shaking, I managed to unbolt it after several tries. Behind me, the invisible footsteps made their way towards me leisurely. The sound of squishing steps amplified my terror, but I was out of the door before they could reach me.

I slipped on my way down the stairs, and my body rolled towards the floor. My chin hit the edge of the last step, tearing open my sensitive skin. Stars danced in front of my eyes due to pain, but I couldn't stop. I needed to get out of the house. The thought was the only thing that urged my limbs into action.

As I passed the living room, I skidded to a stop in terror. A three-tiered wedding cake stood on the kitchen counter, with dead butter-flies decorating it. One side of it was chopped off, and flies buzzed around it. Surrounding it was the decayed food placed between the gasoline-scented candles as if in preparation for a feast.

The spirit haunting me was sick. He wanted to marry me. Or maybe, in his twisted mind, I was already his wife.

I rushed towards the front door. Now, there was a renewed urgency in my steps. I flew out of the front door, grasping my purse and car keys on my way out. I was in my car and reversing it when I looked at the house one last time.

There was a dark shadow standing in the doorway. Its hands were in its pockets, back leaning against the door as if it knew it was going to win. As if it was going to enjoy chasing me.

I repressed the shudder that traveled down my spine and reveled in the sound of tires squealing as I peeled out of the driveway. I was at the end of the street when the sound of a deep laughter reached me. The chase was on, I realized with dread.

I stand at the altar with a dried orange blossoms bouquet in my hands. Dead honeybees and other insects cling to the petals like dew drops. The stink from the candles burning in the demolished church sting my eyes, and I blink away the tears.

I've run for months, with no rest. Finally, I'm out of money and support. Exorcists have refused to help me because they're afraid of it. It's bound to me; that's what they've told me. I freed it from its prison during one of my hikes, and there's nothing in this world that can shield me from it.

I clutch the dagger that I carry in the pockets of the tattered wedding gown that I wear when I hear footsteps I've become familiar with. I listen to them in my nightmares and the familiar stink that overbears all my senses when he gets too close. Sometimes, I feel the whisper of cold bony fingers sliding down my skin when I'm too exhausted to fight. I can't always see him, but I sure as hell can feel his presence.

One way or another, I'm going to end our ill-fated relationship. Today or tomorrow, only one of us will walk the earth again.

SANTA

By Joseph C. Gioconda

"**M**aybe he's on another one of his benders," Alex said. "You know how Jimmy gets this time of year."

"Yeah, I always thought he has that thing—what's it called?" asked Kira, peering into the oven.

"What thing?"

"You know, where you get depressed during the holidays because it's dark outside?" She stood up and took a sip of Chardonnay.

"Depression?" he asked.

"Well, yeah, but it has a specific name," she said.

"Oh, yeah. Seasonal affective disorder. S.A.D. Perfect name."

"Yeah, maybe he has S.A.D. I mean, you get that way during the wintertime. Same genes and all."

"We're not the same in every way," Alex frowned.

"Thank God. I'd never put up with you drinking and partying like him. Neither did Fran."

"I know, but he loves our kids. I think because they never had any before she left, he sees ours as his own," said Alex. "They love him, plus he buys them the most expensive gifts."

"Oh God, is he doing the Santa thing again?" she asked.

"You know it. Dresses up every year. Tries to outdo himself every year. Remember two years ago, when he rented a reindeer?"

"Of course, I do. He is crazy. Well, at least he has the beer belly to pull it off. Doesn't even need padding," she said.

"Come on, be nice; that's my twin you're talking about." He patted his own stomach.

"When's he coming over?"

"I don't know, probably later," Alex said. "Usually, he stops by before Christmas Eve, but I haven't even heard from him in days. By the way, I thought the propane tank was empty. The fire wouldn't light last night."

"You better get it filled! We need a fire on Christmas," she said.

"It's full. I called the gas company, and they came over yesterday and said it's full."

"That's strange because when I tried to light it yesterday morning, it kept going out too," she said.

"I know, I had the same problem this morning. Let me check into it."

"Ok, well, do it *pronto*," she said. "I have dinner on, and your parents get here in a few minutes. Michelle and Evan want to open the rest of their presents."

"Ok. I just texted Jimmy again. No response."

"Ugh." Kira yanked the metal tray containing a large ham out of the oven and put it on the countertop.

The doorbell rang. Michelle and Evan raced to the door to open it.

"Grandma! Grandpa!" they shouted, hugging the elderly couple, who were holding tall stacks of wrapped presents.

"Hi, kids!" The grandparents kissed and hugged them while walking in and dropping the presents down under the tree. "Merry Christmas!"

"What's that smell?" asked Shirley, looking around. She hadn't even taken her coat off. "Smells like something's burning."

"I just took the ham out of the oven," said Kira, giving her a kiss on the cheek. "And I roasted the brussels sprouts, so you probably smell that."

"No, it smells funny. It's not your ham or brussels sprouts," said Shirley.

"I smell it too," said Frank, walking in the front door and removing his scarf and hat and sniffing the air.

"What's it smell like?" asked Kira.

"Smells like… burning hair. And rotting meat."

Kira rolled her eyes.

"What? I don't smell anything," said Alex.

"Maybe because you've been in the house, and we just walked in. We both smell it," said Frank.

Kira looked at her husband. His parents were always creating drama around the holidays, it seemed.

"Never mind. I'll look into it," said Kira. "Come inside and sit down! I am just putting the appetizers out."

"Thank God, I'm starving," said Frank, walking into the family room and rubbing his hands. "What? No fire! It's Christmas for God's sake! Put it on!"

"I know, I know," said Alex. "I'm having some problems lighting it. I checked the fuel gauge. The propane tank is full. I don't know what's wrong with it."

"That's why we use real wood in ours. Reliable! Not like these gas insert logs that are always breaking," said Frank derisively.

"Where's Jimmy?" asked Shirley, already holding an olive on a toothpick.

"I don't know," said Alex. "I called him and got put straight into voicemail. I texted him over the last two days and got no response."

Frank looked at Shirley. "I hope he's not in Vegas. After what he pulled two years ago."

"He's not going back there on Christmas," said Alex. "He promised."

"I have an idea," said Frank. "Do you still have those sticks behind your shed? And the bonfire logs I got you?"

"Yeah, why?" asked Alex.

"Turn off the propane at the source. We'll light a real fire. A Yule log, they call it!"

"Fine, Dad. One more thing off my to-do list," muttered Alex, walking out into the yard from the side entrance. He noticed a familiar car parked on the street in front of their house. It was Jimmy's. He must be sitting inside, smoking a cigarette or something. Alex shook his head and trudged through the snow to the shed. He grabbed a bonfire log by the rope and some kindling and carried the wood outside.

As he walked back into the house, he remembered that he needed to turn off the propane. He dropped the wood by the back door and trudged over to the other side of the building, where the large cylindrical white propane tank was located. He noticed his yellow ladder was propped up against the side of the house.

"What the hell?" he muttered under his breath. He figured the gas company must have borrowed it earlier, needing it to check the chimney and forgotten to put it back in the shed afterward. He left it there and made a mental note to put it back in the shed later.

He carried the wood into the house and dropped it on the gray slate in front of the fireplace grate.

"Jimmy's here," he announced.

"Where is he?" asked Shirley.

"His car's parked on the street. He's probably smoking a cigarette and talking on the phone to his new girlfriend," said Alex.

"Hussies," said Shirley. "All he dates now are hussies."

Alex rolled his eyes. "Merry Christmas to you too, Mom."

He moved the grate away from the fireplace and placed the bonfire log on the metal rack. He put the dry kindling branches underneath it and lit them with a long lighter. The kindling caught.

"There we go. Give it a few minutes to get started," said Alex. "Honey, can you pour me a drink?"

"Spiced rum cider?" Kira asked.

"Now you're talking," he said, peeling off his gloves. "Dad, you want some?"

"Sure, thanks." Frank took a mug of cider from Alex and sipped it. "This is beautiful. Now we have a real fire, the kids are going to open our presents. Ham is ready to be carved. Now, all we need is your brother."

"Let me go get him," said Alex, putting his gloves back on and walking out the front door.

He trudged across the snow-covered lawn to the beat-up car parked on the street in front of their house. He stopped a few yards away when he realized no one was inside of it. Outside of it were three crushed beer cans on the ground.

"Huh," he said under his breath. He figured he must have missed his brother having gone through the garage or around to the back door. He was now even more afraid Jimmy had shown up drunk again.

He walked back inside.

"Where is he?" asked Alex.

"What do you mean?" Frank asked Alex. "Didn't you go out to get him?"

"Yeah, he isn't in his car," said Alex.

"He didn't come in here," said Shirley.

"Could he have gone for a walk?" asked Frank.

"In the snow?" asked Alex. "Doubt it. Plus, I didn't see footprints."

Just then, the rancid smell of burning, rotting meat, hair, and rubber started to fill the room.

"Jesus, what the hell is that awful smell?" asked Frank. "That's like what we smelled earlier. Worse, actually."

"I think something's caught in the chimney," said Alex. "Let me look."

He pulled the grate away and tried to see what was obstructing the flue. Jimmy's black rubber Santa boot fell into the fire.

42

VELES

A Lovecraftian Poem by Petar Vrbich

I shall seek greatness in that which is filled with shortcomings.

I shall seek happiness in that which is sorrowful.

I shall seek Veles in thou depths, for he hides outside
of where he should dwell—in our world.

The times have passed throughout which the great serpent
slithered upon us, humans. The time has come for him to return.
To bring them shortcomings, sorrow, and death. To grant
me greatness, happiness, and eternal life. I, forever a servant
to him, but a servant worthy, I will release my master.

To begin I went, sought, found, and took. She, very much human and
alive, warm, and fearful, making it perfect, making it as he would
wish. Cry I say, cry and rest upon thy underworld, I am releasing
you of these Earthly bonds and the terror which will unfold. Feast
upon my dagger, slit thou throat I shall, make you be the last one

to join the promised land, the last one to pass the gates of Hell
until something far worse comes, something he and I will bring.

Oh, Veles. Thy horn is my grail! Oh, mighty dragon, live
within us now, for I summon you this woman. I gift you
her carnal flesh and blood, for please, come among us.

Chodź, ojcze, wężu lasu, weź to stado i
przynieś ten świat ze sobą world.

·

(Come, oh father, snake of the woods, take this
herd and bring your world with you.)

I chant, oh thy greatness, I beg now, come,
release yourself from thy chains!

Chodź, ojcze, wężu lasu, weź to stado i
przynieś ten świat ze sobą world.

As the rain pours and the thunder strikes the trees behind me,
the thick forest becomes misty, ready for his reincarnation.
He is coming; he is coming to take the beasts. Veles shall
strike you all down and attach you to his herd!

The horned scaly snake, meters upon meters long, with golden
crowns spreading across his body, now is here. Every horn, carrying
a star, there are ten of them, intertwined one into another. Of
black color they are, and the face underneath them, of gold and
obsidian, with two large emeralds, looking deep into my soul.
His coat, now flowing effortlessly in the air, like gravitation
there is not. His hands, special for a serpent, with perfect spheres
in each, create and destroy life, so powerful and perfect.

I released you, oh great godly beast! I gave
life, oh my lord, take me with you!

He looks now at me, researching my body and my mind.
I feel his wrath deep in my chest. I feel the existence of
the power, the never-ending flames, and his godly form.
Like thousand needles stabbing me, yet so gentle and
easy. Like leeches attached to me, he seeks me out.

Show me the underworld!

I beg, for I do not wish to see what he does to the world, now
unleashed and ready to swallow. I enter his domain, through the
pathway formed, a bridge into another world, already blunt and dark,
cold, and long, with no barriers, just an open void, in which anything
could come. A humid, fleshy tone I smell, spreads across my skin.
Breathing is hard; existing feels unreal. There are things here, I see
them in the distance, red as molten iron, they approach me. I look
around the void, which resembles a cave. The unknown stars in the
distance, all of them which humanity could have reached, are now
forgotten, and seen by me only. I am inside him; I am truly inside
the old god, and it is home. They are even closer now, as I do not
know what they are, so red and seems beautiful. The lights perhaps I
should call them. They are full of tentacles, fire in between each one,
flames. That must be the soul of the god, perhaps one which every
god has. I have come to the absolute core; I have come to the master's
domain. The fortune I have brought upon myself, oh, how great it is!

Imagine just how one must now be swallowing the Earth. Rising
in front of all those unloyal men, behold now, planet Earth, a
god has come. There is no one to stop him, there is no one to save
you, there is only me within him and he, Veles the almighty, a

serpent which shall bind you in his tail. You shall join me here to look at the lights endlessly, as I am your owner, and he is mine. Are you ready to receive the punishment? Is humanity ready for the battle of the ones which are not of that world? For the end?

And to them now, wondering the realms of men, the great small of earthly substances emerged in the air. Filled their lungs and crystalized in them. So dead and old, a smell which screams demise. That is what they shall feel, as any of the forms of Veles materializes around them. Then, slowly, amid darkness, taking their body and soul, to the realms of thy unknown and terrifying. A sight to take in, one which would drive any normal individual to madness, making him numb to all emotions and feelings. Creating nothing out of something, perhaps a property of a God stronger than those of creating something out of nothing. For why create when it could be destroyed?

And after those events, the world shall seek rebirth, a state where nature will prevail. Complete absence of all civilization and human life, those which ruined it so bad.

That is what I sought, and that is what is deemed to become the truth. The serpent is now here. The grand plan is achieved.

I will now rest, as I enter the redness which is overcoming my ability to see and perceiving. I am the soul within the soul, as I now enter, Veles.

I found greatness in shortcomings.

I found happiness in sorrow.

I found Veles.

CONFESSION

By Joseph C. Gioconda

"**D**id you do anything to hurt these people?"

"I wished death and injury upon them, Father."

"No, I understand that. I mean, did you pull the trigger? Did you engage in any actions?"

"My intention *was* the action. That's what I am trying to explain," said the young man. "Whenever I want something terrible to happen to someone, it just happens. That's how I get ahead in life. I'm somehow rewarded for making these terrible thoughts real."

He kneeled in an old wooden confessional in St. Mel's parish. He had driven fifty miles away from his hometown to avoid the risk of confessing to a priest who might recognize his voice. He had never been in this church before, and even though he knew that priests were under a strict duty to never reveal what they hear in confession, he couldn't take any chances. Especially after the last one.

But he needed to be absolved. He needed catharsis. He really didn't want to sin again, even though he suspected he probably would.

"You have serious thoughts of harming others?" the priest asked.

"Yes, I wish them harm. I want them to die insufferable, tragic deaths."

"Why would you want that?" asked the priest.

"It started when I was bullied as a freshman. I was only thirteen, and a kid in my high school class was cruel to me. His name was Chuck. He nicknamed me 'forky,' because I had forked front teeth, and my parents couldn't afford to get me braces. Once the nickname caught on, it destroyed my self-esteem. I stopped going out after school; I would just hide in my basement and play video games alone. I had no friends; I was really depressed."

"That's very challenging," the priest said.

"I started to pray that Chuck would die," the young man whispered. "I really, really wanted him to. I prayed for it with all my might. If he died, I figured, I would be spared this endless torture at school. From the minute that I woke up to the minute I fell asleep, I wished death upon him."

"Did you seek counseling?"

"No. I spent all my energy wishing for it to happen."

"So, what happened?"

"They found his body in the forest behind the high school. He had been stabbed eighty-one times."

The priest paused.

"Did you have something to do with that?"

"Yes, I wished it upon him," he whispered.

"I mean, did you kill Chuck because of the nickname he bestowed upon you?"

"I wished he would die, I admit that. But I had nothing physically to do with his death. But in the days and weeks that followed, once I was cleared of any wrongdoing, I got my life back."

"How so?"

"Well, even though I had a rock-solid alibi, I think the other kids just assumed I did it somehow. I started to seem like a badass, even though I was not involved with the murder. It was apparently a drug-related murder. My social standing went up. Girls started to notice me. I started to dress better. Got a little more confidence. No one ever called me 'forky' again."

"You must understand you aren't even remotely responsible for Chuck's death. You were suffering, and you wished him harm, I understand that. But you aren't morally responsible for his death if you didn't do it."

"But it didn't stop there, Father. I wish it had."

"What happened?"

"Well, I got up enough confidence to ask a girl out on a date. Her name was Samantha. She was beautiful. Long straight blonde hair, gorgeous smile. She said no. But she didn't just say no. She mocked me. She laughed in my face and told all her friends what a loser I was. She told me she'd never go out with a freak show like me."

"That's awful. Kids can be very cruel."

"So, I became even crueler."

"What did you do?"

"I did the same thing I did with Chuck. But this time, I was more specific and didn't want her to die. I wanted her to suffer. So, I started playing out little scenarios in my head."

"Did you hurt her physically?"

"No. But about a week later, after I started my prayers, she was in a terrible car accident. She didn't die, but her face and body were so mangled and burnt. She is a vegetable. She will never walk again, and even if she did, she would never want to look in the mirror."

"That's really sad," said the priest.

"It is, but again, I benefitted. People started whispering, and I got even more popular somehow. Samantha's friend Brittany asked *me* out."

"And you think that had something to do with these tragedies?"

"I know it did."

"How?"

"Well, I think that I was somehow being rewarded for my evil thoughts."

"Was that the only two instances? Chuck and Samantha?"

"Not by a long shot."

"What do you mean?"

"No less than eight more."

"Eight more what?" the priest asked.

"Tragedies."

"And you had nothing to do with any of them?"

"As I said before, not directly, not physically. But as my powers grew, the stakes went up. The more specific I was in my prayers, the more accurate it was. And then I started getting really rewarded. I won a small lottery prize after another enemy of mine was killed drunk driving. Took home fifteen thousand dollars. Got a full ride scholarship to college after another died in a car crash when his brakes failed."

"Do you want to hear my advice?"

"Yes, Father."

"I think the only sin you've committed is inside your head and heart. I don't think you had anything whatsoever to do with any of these sad, terrible tragedies. You only wish you did because it gives you a false sense of power. If you committed any sin, it's the sin of pride. It's a purely internal sin, one that can lead to worse things. But if you never actually picked up a knife or gun, or cut someone's brake lines, or made them drive drunk, I don't see how God would hold you accountable for these tragedies. They happen. People die. It's not your fault. But one last question."

"Yes, Father?"

"Are you sorry? For whatever you believe that you did wrong, are you sorry?"

"No."

"You aren't?"

"No, I wish I was. I came here seeking absolution and consolation. I want to feel sorry. But now that I recount these things, I realize that I'm not sorry. I am thankful. I am just glad I have these powers."

"I have a recommendation," said the priest. "I think you really need therapy. That is beyond my authority to offer that to you here, but I think you should sit down with a licensed psychiatrist or psychoanalyst to get to the bottom of why you feel so powerless."

"Powerful, you mean."

"Well, I think you desperately want the feeling of power," said the priest. "But you are actually powerless, and that's what's driving this desire to harm others and benefit somehow from their suffering."

"I disagree, Father."

"Ok, well, I don't think I can help you any further. If you sincerely aren't sorry for whatever sins you think you committed, I can't absolve you. If you were truly sorry, I would, but like I said, I think this is more of a mental health issue than one of sin and forgiveness."

"So, you won't absolve me?"

"I don't think so, no."

The man was silent.

"You drive a Volvo, Father?"

"What?"

"Your car. Is it a Volvo?"

"Why do you ask?"

"Father Altstadt drove one too."

The priest heard the young man step out of the confessional and walk out the back door toward the parking lot. He remembered that his friend Father Altstadt had died in a fiery car wreck last month.

11

BABYSITTING

By Sarah Putnam Ropes

When I was a senior in high school, I made a little extra money on the side babysitting for our neighbors' daughter. They lived in an old house down the block, and they would pay me in cash for their regular 'date night.'

Since Emmy was one of the sweetest, nicest kids you could think of, I didn't mind sacrificing a Friday or Saturday night to make a hundred bucks since I could just sit on my iPhone and text with my friends. The parents were usually home by midnight, so I could even still go out with my boyfriend if I wanted to sneak out and get home a little late.

Their house was set up so that there was a long hallway from the living room area that led all the way to the back of the house, where the bedrooms and bathroom were located. This layout allowed me to sit on the couch and look down the hallway and see Emmy's bedroom as well as the hallway bathroom.

Anyway, it was about 10:30 p.m. one night, and I had already put Emmy to bed and was just texting with my friends while I was sitting on their couch. I heard footsteps run down the hall to the bathroom. I assumed it was Emmy going to the bathroom, which was a little weird because she had already gone to the toilet before I put her to bed. I didn't turn and look up from my iPhone.

A few minutes went by, and I heard the same footsteps heading back down the hall toward her bedroom. I turned and looked up to tell her that she hadn't flushed the toilet, and I didn't hear her wash her hands. I saw the tips of long jet-black hair scurry past the open doorway into her bedroom.

Here's the problem: Emmy is blonde.

I frantically jumped up and raced to Emmy's bedroom and threw open her door. Her nightlight was on, and it was bright enough for me to see her sit up in bed and look at me while rubbing her eyes in confusion.

I asked her, "Did you just go to the bathroom?"

She shook her head. I did a once over of her room, checking under her bed and quickly peeking in her closet. I didn't see anyone and told Emmy I was just double-checking everything, so I wouldn't freak her out. But I had clearly seen a figure with black hair walking into her room only moments ago.

I tucked her back into bed and said good night again, heading back out of her room. I stopped at the doorway and heard her whisper, thinking she was going to ask me for something like a drink of water before I left.

Instead, I overheard her say to someone, "Don't scare her again; I really like her."

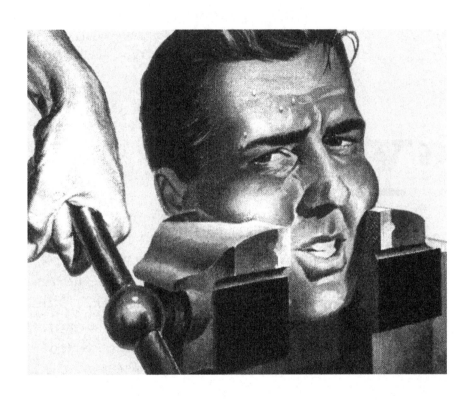

INVENTOR

By Joseph C. Gioconda

"**Y**ou already own a patent?"

"Several, actually."

"All in the same field?"

"In one form or another."

The two men sat across a large marble table in an opulent conference room in Palo Alto, California. John Owens, the elder named partner at the law firm, had agreed to meet Thomas Song, a prospective client. The lawyer wore a sharp pinstriped suit, while his new client wore a tattered t-shirt and stained jeans. His awkward appearance didn't faze the lawyer. Many of his successful clients in Silicon Valley were eccentric but had made millions inventing novel software applications.

The firm's paralegal had taken notes about Mr. Song's professed legal needs, which included filing several new patent applications, as well as taking over a substantial portfolio of pending and issued ones. The man had also apparently asked if Owens' firm had criminal defense counsel on staff, which the paralegal thought was an odd question. Therefore, given the nature of the notes, the lawyer decided to leave the young paralegal out of today's conversation with the man and handle the consultation himself.

"Please tell me a little about your business," Owens asked Song while pouring coffee into a mug.

"My business is my own."

Owens raised an eyebrow, putting the mug down after stirring it. "I don't understand what you mean."

"How I make a living isn't relevant to these inventions," Song said curtly.

"Well, that may be true, Mr. Song, but the United States Patent and Trademark Office will ask about the commercial utility of your... inventions," the lawyer said, flipping through the detailed drawings, diagrams, and photographs the man had brought in neatly labeled manila folders. "By the way, do we have your inventor's notebooks for each of these?"

"I keep copious journals in bound composition books," Song said.

"Good, we will need to keep coming back to those to understand how exactly you conceived these ideas, reduced them to practice, and built prototypes." The lawyer flipped to the first detailed sketch and text.

"Device for the treatment of hiccups," Owens read aloud. "Sounds interesting..." The lawyer read from the description:

> *The present invention generally relates to a device for the treatment of hiccups, and more specifically, to a method and apparatus for treating hiccups involving galvanic stimulation of the Superficial Phrenetic and Vagus nerves.*

"And what was the impetus behind this one?"

"I was in a movie theater," Song said. "A man in front of me had hiccups. It spoiled the entire film. I kept asking him to cease. He apologized and said he couldn't. But he wouldn't leave. I needed to invent something to solve the problem. The exact anatomic and physiological mechanism responsible for causing hiccups remains unknown, you know."

"Uh, no, I didn't know that. Please continue."

"The idea is that this invention will put a human head into a vise, and a metal vessel will cover the person's mouth and nose completely."

The lawyer looked the inventor up and down and continued reading.

> When the vessel is filled with an electrically conductive potable liquid, such as tap water, the electrodes are immersed in the liquid. The second electrode is also configured so as to contact the temple and cheek region of the face when drinking liquids from the cup-like vessel. During typical human oral consumption of the liquid from the lip of the cup-like vessel of the present invention, an electrical circuit is created, and the electro-chemically produced potential energy, or ions, are conducted through the electrodes and the electro-conductive liquid to the user's lips, mouth, and throat as well as the temple region of the face, thus stimulating the superficially coursing vagus and phrenic nerves and reliably interrupting the hiccup reflexive arc.

"So, you want to put their head in a vise and electrocute them?" the lawyer said, looking up at him, horrified.

"Electroshock therapy works, counselor."

"You aren't joking? Are there any references to prior art? Previous inventions that did anything remotely similar?"

"Just one, and it is old and very, very different. I think this one will sail through and get immediate approval."

"Ok, what about this second one, 'The Human Wash'?"

"People are filthy," Song said. "Homeless degenerates complain that it's too difficult to take a bath or shower every day. I personally wash five times a day. But the people I smell on the train clearly do not. The idea here is that vagrants or patients in a nursing home can stand or sit on a conveyor belt while they are washed. Think of a human car wash."

The lawyer stared at the man. "Let me read your proposed description of this one."

Institutional patients who spend any material amount of time in bed are likely to be susceptible to fungus and skin disease infection in the buttocks, the thighs, and the hairy portions of the body. In controlling the spread of contagious skin diseases in institutions, it is these very portions of the body which need to be bathed most frequently and most thoroughly, but it is very difficult for either the patients or the institutional attendants to reach these portions of the body with soap and water when the patients are bathed in a sitting position.

The lawyer looked back up at him over his eyeglasses.

"Again, any prior art?" he asked.

"Very few machines do this," said the inventor. "They do not come close to addressing the necessity here."

"Not surprising," said the lawyer. "And lastly, you call this one 'The Baby Cage.' Care to explain this one?"

"The poor live in squalid apartments. Their babies are stuck in these damp, dark places. They need to be exposed to air and sunlight. Sometimes, parents put their babies on the fire escape. This leads to falls, often fatal. So, I concocted a contraption that allows babies to sit in a cage that has bamboo grates, attached to the outside of the window on a high floor."

"You propose putting children in a tiger cage?"

"It's not a tiger cage. It's a way to keep children safe and healthy."

"Let me understand this, Mr. Song. You want a patent on an invention to put children in cages to hang them out of windows?"

"The structures can be metal, but the bars get too hot in the blazing sun. That is an alternative embodiment if you read the whole application, but yes, bamboo is preferred."

"Mr. Song," the lawyer said, closing the folder. "I don't think I can represent you. These applications are not only commercially ridiculous, but I also don't see how they are feasible to even propose. Frankly, they are nothing more than bizarre torture devices that would raise eyebrows at the Patent Office, as well as my law firm. I don't even understand how you created prototypes to test them out."

"Again, that is my business."

"Wait, so you tried these things out?!"

"A good inventor needs to make many mistakes before he perfects an idea. Isn't that what Edison said? 'I didn't fail in inventing the light bulb; I discovered a thousand ways not to.' My inventions now work, after much trial and error."

The man handed the lawyer a marble composition book and a folder containing glossy photographs. They were stained with bloody fingerprints on the edges.

"It took many tries to get that man to stop hiccupping. But when the vise was tightened enough, and I found the right voltage and amperage, he stopped. And the human wash, well, the homeless appreciate it. Of course, the water must be scalding to get the skin, dirt, and lice all off, and it must be used five times a day, so they must be chained to the chairs. And as for the cages, they're still being tested. Failures are inevitable, counselor. Trial and error."

13

SONG

by Isabel Rincón

"Why don't you try it out?" she says, hands hidden behind her back, "I'm sure you'll be convinced then."

Lucas scratches his chin, his fingernails scraping against the stubble that he forgot to shave yesterday, and gazes at the piano in the middle of the store. It's a baby grand, its wood irregularly reddish in color, brown under certain angles. The piano would go nicely in the living room of the apartment that he's renting now. There's certainly enough space for it, but his budget is another issue altogether. The tempting old spinet on the corner sells for a much lower price, considering the substantial drop in sound quality.

His other hand clenches. He's been practicing on a keyboard that a friend loaned him for the past few weeks to save enough money to move from the flat he shared with five more guys. He's on his own now. He got a raise at his day job, so getting a real instrument for practice is a 'now or never' kind of deal.

Not that a keyboard isn't a real instrument, Lucas corrects himself internally. He's heard enough about that from his friend, and he was kind enough to do him such a big favor, so Lucas has learned to keep his opinions to himself.

He shakes his head. "I fear that if I give it a try, I won't want to stop."

She smiles, a gesture that doesn't quite reach her eyes. Lucas finds nothing weird in it; he used to work in sales before, he knows how soul-draining it is to smile. He tries corresponding with a friendly shrug and sits in front of it on the soft leathery bench that creaks under his weight. He takes a moment to admire his reflection on the polished wood.

"C'mon, it's not going to bite you." She takes a couple of steps and comes to stand right behind him. Her perfume reaches his nose. It's cheap and makes him want to cough.

"It's just... been a while since I had a grand right in front of me. Wanted to go back to recitals, y'know? I used to love playing for an audience." The heat of the stage lights, the amplitude and never-ending darkness at the other side of them. He knows there are people there, countless of eyes and ears giving Lucas their full attention, but he can't look back at them. The feeling of being the one thing that hungry darkness craves for can't be compared to anything else.

"Sir? Are you listening to me?" She asks.

Lucas is brought back to reality after drifting into places he hasn't visited in years. "Sorry, Miss. So! The piano, yes. Let's see."

His hands firmly raise the fallboard to reveal rows of white under interrupted rows of black. The ivory keys welcome him, and Lucas can't contain himself. A finger presses one of them, and the note that comes out echoes all around the music store's walls.

"Oh, wow, either the acoustics are incredible here, or this is a damn fine piano. Oh! Sorry." He cringes at the swear word that escapes from his lips, which makes her giggle.

The sound, like chimes in the wind, sends a shiver down Lucas' spine. He pushes the feeling away and, to try and lighten the mood, plays *Mary Had a Little Lamb,* focusing on the image of the piano strings being hammered one by one as he does.

"It likes you."

"Huh?" Lucas turns around.

"The piano, it likes you." With a quick and elegant gesture, she tucks a strand of hair behind an ear. "It wouldn't sound this good if it didn't. You have to take it with you."

Lucas knows he's visibly cringing at her words; as much as he loves music, he'd never think about speaking about a tool in that way. The kind of people that do are better kept at arms' distance, in his opinion, as they tend to be incredibly intense in his experience. He agrees with her in any case—the piano sound just right—and before he realizes it, his credit card is on the counter, and a payment plan is being set.

Back at home, Lucas begins moving furniture around to make space for his latest acquisition. Will it like to be by the window? Or would it prefer to be closer to the door, where it stays warm during the winter?

As he pulls a stack of empty cardboard boxes, Lucas can't help but laugh at himself for doing exactly what he had criticized before. He chooses to make the piano the focus point of his living room, angling the secondhand couch and plastic chairs in the direction of the currently empty space.

The only thing left is to put the old keyboard away. Lucas fully plans on giving it back, but he stores it in his closet for the time being until his friend finally picks up the phone.

"So weird," Lucas muses out loud in bed, "he never separates from the damned thing but hasn't read even one of my texts." The only reply he gets is silence, as expected, and he sets a mental reminder to thank his friend for telling him about the music store whenever one of his calls gets picked up.

The following day comes with little to no ceremony. Lucas goes to work, types mindlessly on his office's computer, prints papers, does some tech support for non-tech-savvy people, and dies a little bit inside with every minute that passes. He swears that he's going to implode if he must ask if the client has tried to turn on and off their device. It's so monotonous that Lucas only thinks about the piano during his lunch hour and wonders why the store hasn't called to set a delivery time.

He takes out his phone and dials their number. An automated voice blasts against his ear. "We're sorry," the message says, "the number you're trying to reach has been disconnected or is no longer in service."

"Weird." Lucas takes a bite of the cold chicken sandwich he brought with him. It tastes as good as the day is going for him.

He chooses to deal with the delivery when he gets home. When he finally does, after dragging his feet up the stairs because the elevator isn't working, he's welcomed by a tall and wide box in front of his door. The sticker on it has the music store's logo, the contact number that he tries calling, and Lucas' address. He has no recollection of ever sharing all that information, now that he thinks about it, but the excitement stops any sort of logical thinking, and Lucas brings the heavy box into his apartment.

The box gets opened with the same energy a child would use to unwrap a Christmas gift, and Lucas' hands are trembling by the time he's pulling away the last piece of plastic covering between the instrument and himself. Before he places it in the space he made for it, Lucas presses some of the keys, letting out a content sigh once the pleasurable sound reaches his ears. The piano, which appeared at his place out of pretty much nowhere, is tuned.

Lucas can't wait, so he sits in the middle of his living room, takes a second to admire the feel and smell of the beautiful wooden casing; it exudes a strange, metallic aroma that he's never sensed in any other similar instrument but Lucas concludes it must come from being transported in a truck and plays for the rest of the day. The last time he felt this level of happiness was when he was a child attending music classes, when he practiced for recitals, and maybe, just maybe, when he got his first kiss. Bach and Tchaikovsky flow from his fingers with ease, as some things can't be forgotten once learned. Lucas believes he hears one of his neighbors bang against their ceiling to make him stop, but he ignores that and keeps going, possibly playing louder.

The next day, he calls in sick to work, feigning a cough that would make any respectable actor or lazy student scoff at the sorry excuse for an interpretation. Lucas hasn't moved the piano, doesn't think he will, and busies himself with perusing his sheets to pick which piece he's going to try next.

"Debussy sounds like a great option, don't you think?" Lucas asks the piano. "It's my friend's favorite."

The piano doesn't reply, nor does it need to. Lucas shrugs and lets himself sink into the images of a scenario surrounded by hot, white lights, the picture of an ocean of darkness behind all of that. He's young again, dressed in his best clothes, and the reddish wood of the piano, which looks darker today than it did yesterday, morphs into a longer, more exposed form.

Minutes turn into hours, and hours turn into days. Eventually, his phone's battery dies, and the calls from work stop coming. Someone knocks on his door, either today, maybe tomorrow, but for Lucas, there's only the ache in his fingers, the tension and release of his muscles when he steps on the pedals, or his hands travel from one extreme of the keyboard to the other. His soul slides over a road of ivory and ebony steps, descending further into the sensations that cloud a reality that will never fulfill him like this.

And then his stomach rumbles; his body has different needs and a will of its own. Lucas doubles down and is surprised by the intense ache in his middle. When was the last time he ate anything? He charges his phone, turns it on, and curses when he sees the date. Two days have passed, and Lucas' throat feels drier than ever. He drinks a glass of water as waves of notifications start coming in, making his phone buzz repeatedly. Most of them are the missed calls from works, unwanted texts, and boring news, so he swipes them away, orders a pizza, and flexes his strained hands.

The tips of his fingers are crusty with something brown. Lucas brings then to his face and detects the characteristic smell of dried blood. His eyes dart to the piano; the keys are covered by dots of the same substance that look like the wood in color. He washes his hands and the piano's keys with a rag. As he does that, a food delivery guy rings his doorbell. Lucas throws a couple of ten-dollar bills at the guy, who is taken aback when he sees Lucas' face.

"You, uh, have something here." He points under Lucas' nose and leaves after whispering "weirdo."

Lucas scratches his face and realizes that, at some point during the previous days, his nose had bled.

"What a mess." He cleans himself up, eats a slice of pizza, and puts away the rest for later if he manages to get over how disgusting the idea of eating has become. He doesn't want to consume when he's the one that wants to be consumed by the music.

He goes back to playing, each piece coming back to him as if he had never stopped taking classes and refuses to be distracted by his body again. Time goes on, and Lucas feels something dripping from his nose, the metallic tang dispersing any doubts over what it might be. He keeps going until all sensation is replaced with melodies, until his vision blurs with the red tones of fluid flowing freely, until the skin from his fingers starts peeling back, until his eyes are dry, and his lids won't move.

And even then, he goes on. There's no outside world, there's no outside, there's only the piano that feels familiar in the most terrible but comforting of ways. He's got to thank him, Lucas thinks, his friend, the piano. He's going to thank him, it, with a song.

His body begins giving away, and Lucas must fight against the weakening vessel to make each note follow the previous one. His arms grow heavy, and for the first time in weeks, a word comes out from his lips. "Shit."

She giggles. She's always been here.

"Enjoying your purchase, aren't you?"

Her hand invades Lucas' reduced field of vision and scopes up a handful of his blood.

"Just in time for a new coat of paint."

Her voice drifts as she smears the liquid over the wood unceremoniously; she then turns her head to look back at Lucas.

She's smiling. "Look alive, sir; you're doing us a great favor."

Lucas whimpers, unable to muster the strength to say anything else.

One of his hands gets caught in hers, and she raises it for Lucas to stare at the horror of exposed bone and cartilage.

"These will make great keys, I hope. Your friend's bones weren't up to par with our expectations, but he sent you to us, so it all turned out great in the end."

She lets Lucas go and pats her pencil skirt, shaking the dust off it.

"Why don't you go back to playing while I make a couple of calls? We'll have to drive you and the piano back to the store to finish the process, but it seems that you could give it another go. It likes you more than we expected; that'll make the paint last even longer."

Everything is confusing. Lucas' thoughts run in circles clashing against one another, trying to make sense of the situation. Each attempt is met with failure, so he complies because the piano is welcoming, the music is right, a last song sounds like the greatest idea he's ever heard. He doesn't know what will happen after or if there's even an after.

Her words as she speaks on the phone are muffled by the melody of farewell. He's saying goodbye, but he doesn't know who it is directed at because Lucas and the piano will be one sooner rather than later, and then the music will last through eternity.

When the darkness finally shadows his view, he keeps playing as his body dries.

"He's here," she says, holding the door open.

He's there, until he isn't.

HIKE

By Joseph C. Gioconda

I went to college in a remote location that was far from any major cities or towns, so the thick forests were all around us. My friend Jim and I really enjoyed hiking. There was a serious trail about an hour's drive from the university. We borrowed our friend's car, packed it up with our camping supplies, and drove to the trailhead.

The trail itself was over fifty miles long, so it would take us at least four days to hike in and get back to the car. Now, I am an experienced scout who has spent countless hours in the woods. I went on many backpacking treks throughout my youth, so I was very comfortable with this trip. I was used to the minor 'spooky' things you hear at night in the woods: coyote howls, raccoons, even the occasional unknown noise, which could be a bear or mountain lion. Of course, the scariest thing to find in the deep woods are unexpected people.

Now, this trail was for experienced hikers only. There were warning signs everywhere, and I had read up on it from discussions on the Internet. Many amateur hikers had gone missing in this wilderness, and in fact, a support group had been formed by the families of the missing. But because it was so rugged and remote, few campers made it very far into the forest.

It was the end of the second day, and we were already about twenty-five miles deep into the trail. The underbrush and trees lined the trails densely. We hadn't seen another hiker for many miles, as most had stopped and turned around at the first five-mile point marker. There weren't many signs of people having used the trail lately.

Nonetheless, to set up camp, I always walk at least a hundred meters off the main trail to reduce the chances of my camp disturbing other hikers, or vice-versa. So, Jim and I went off to find this amazing spot well off the trail. It was probably close to two hundred meters off the trail. It was so far away that it would be difficult to even see our flashlights at night.

This spot was also on a peninsula near a major river. Therefore, there was only one way in and one way out to our campsite. We started a campfire, cooked our food, and just chilled out. We put the fire out at midnight and headed back to our respective tents.

It was the fall semester, so crunchy leaves had fallen on the ground, the moon was brightly shining through the trees, and the air was cool. The only noise was the occasional time when I would hear my friend turn over in his sleep. Then, I heard the voices.

They sounded shockingly close for being on a trail two hundred meters away. I checked my watch; it was 3 a.m. Who hikes at 3 a.m., twenty-five miles into deep forest?

I slowly got out of my sleeping bag and unzipped my tent and poked my head out. I saw Jim peeking out of his tent simultaneously. He moved his finger over his mouth as if to say "hush."

Then we saw them. Three men and two women. They were walking directly toward our camp. In the darkness, we could make out that none of them had a backpack, which seemed like an impossibility unless they had all their gear stored somewhere very nearby. They were walking silently at this point. There were no lights illuminating their path, and there was no crunch as they stomped on the dry leaves underfoot. We watched them glide closer and closer.

Jim was the first to speak up and ask what they were doing at our campsite.

At first, they did not answer and just kept approaching us slowly.

I shouted out another question.

"What do you want? Why aren't you using a light? Do you need help finding the trail back?"

The older man, who had a scraggly beard, said, "We don't use lights."

I looked at Jim quizzically. He looked unnerved.

Suddenly, the five people formed a circle around the remnants of our campfire, raised their arms above their heads, and began to chant. They clearly knew English from our earlier exchange, but the language they were singing was not English. In fact, it was no language I had ever heard before. They seemed to exhale the guttural words.

After only a few seconds, all five morphed into a single being. The entity had eyes in random places on its face and body, and it began to scream.

I was paralyzed with fear. I suddenly felt extremely sleepy. I cannot explain it. I had been wired and nerve-wracked by their presence only a few moments ago, yet now I couldn't keep my eyes open to stare at this atrocity.

When I glanced over at Jim, he had a glazed look in his eyes. He pulled his head back into his tent and disappeared into it. I needed to lay my head back down.

When my eyes opened, the sky was bright, and birds were singing.

I crept out of my tent. There was no sign of the creature. I went into his tent and shook Jim awake. I asked what had happened the night before.

He said nothing had happened, but he had a terrifying dream that some kind of demon ghost had visited us in the night and tried to steal our souls. I told him that I didn't think it was a dream as I could remember exactly what the five people that morphed into an amorphous entity looked like and what they had said.

However, his dream was that he had seen a transparent phantom glide into the campsite. After that, he couldn't remember anything.

We packed up, turned around, headed back to the trail, and headed back home. I will never hike again.

15

MAUSOLEUM

By Joseph C. Gioconda

"Robbie, where do you go at night?"

"What do you mean?"

"I mean that I keep finding mud on your sheets and your socks. Maybe you need to see Dr. Lampart if you are blacking out and wandering around at night again."

"Fine, waste your money. He just gives me sleeping pills. I could barely keep my head off my desk at school. In September, that's going to become a problem. Plus, this summer, you know that I need to be at work at seven. I can't oversleep."

"What do you want me to do, chain you to your bed? Is that what you want?" Nancy asked, exasperated.

"At least I'd get a good night's sleep," he muttered.

"Your father and I are concerned about this summer job anyway. Just quit. I'll tell Harold to let you go. We can give you some extra allowance money. You should have enough cash for the summer."

"It's not about the money, Mom. I like the job."

"They're not even paying you minimum wage; did you know that?"

"Yeah, that's only because I'm too young to legally work. I'm fourteen; I couldn't get a job anywhere this summer. Not without working papers," he said.

"Yeah, I know, I got you the job, remember? But that's not the point. Harold's a friend of mine. He puts the ads for his cemetery in the newspaper, I talk to him all the time. I can tell him you're having some personal problems and need to take the rest of the summer off."

"Oh great, that'll go over well. Nicole will love that."

"What do you care what she thinks? She's three years older than you. She's graduating in June."

"You know why."

"Oh, because she's dating Chris Fortunato."

"I want her to dump him and go out with me instead. He's such a loser," Robbie said.

"He's her age. Ok, Ok. Look, your father and I are not going to tell you how to live your life, but I'm concerned if you're sleepwalking or wandering around the streets at night. It's dangerous."

"I know, Mom," he said.

"And what's this?" She held up a large iron key with a cross inside. It had an ornate letter 'A' on it.

"Where'd you find that?" Robbie said, snatching it out of her hand.

"In your jeans," his mother said. "It was all muddy, too."

"It looks like maybe something from work. I don't remember picking it up. Forget about it. Thanks." He put the key in his poncho. "I gotta get to work now."

Robbie walked to work in the pouring rain.

"Look at this guy," Christopher joked as the two boys stood at the front gate to the cemetery next to the maintenance shed to start their grueling day. "I thought you'd have quit this crappy job by now."

"Why would you think that?" asked Robbie.

"I thought you'd be soft. But you're here, so I give you credit."

"Yeah, a lot of good that'll do me," Robbie said. "Today's a total washout."

"I know. I'll tell Harold later we couldn't work in torrential rain. He doesn't get into work until ten, though," said Chris. "We have to at least try to get something done. Damn, I forgot to clock us in."

"I'll do it," said Robbie, walking into the shed and clocking himself in. "How's Nicole?"

"She's great," said Christopher. "She thinks she has it tough working at the perfume counter at Sterns! Can you believe that primadonna? We got our faces in the rain and mud here, she's spraying rich women with perfume in air conditioning at the mall, and she's the one complaining. She doesn't even have to be to work until noon."

"Hah, yeah," said Robbie, downplaying his interest in Chris' girlfriend.

"Now, let's get to work," Chris said, turning the ignition on the back-hoe they used to dig the new graves. "This is going to be a total mess."

"Hey," Robbie yelled to him through the wind and rain.

"Yeah?" Chris responded, wiping the rainwater out of his eyes.

"Isn't today your birthday?"

"Yeah," Chris laughed. "Great way to spend it, huh?"

"I have a little present for you," Robbie said. "You recognize this?" He pulled the rusty key out of his jeans and showed it to Chris, who took it from him. The rain dripped off the key.

"Holy shit, where'd you find this?"

"Remember you told me about those old mausoleums up on the hill?" asked Robbie.

"The abandoned ones?" asked Chris.

"Yeah. Well, one of them has this exact letter 'A' on the iron bars, with the name Amontillado. Well, I went inside and found something beautiful that you could give Nicole. Let me show you, hop in the back of the cart. We're not getting any work done in this weather anyway."

Robbie jumped in the driver's seat of the golf cart, turning it on and driving them up the winding paved road to the north of the graveyard, which snaked up a steep hill. They passed a natural lake, which was overflowing from the runoff.

"Wow, the lake is flooding; you don't see that often," said Chris. "My Dad told me it's a deep natural spring they used to quarry these headstones; I heard it's over a hundred feet down."

We have to get out here and walk," said Robbie, parking the golf cart. "It's too muddy and steep to use this thing," he said.

They got out of the cart and trudged up the muddy embankment.

"I call this Bone Hill," said Chris. "It's actually called Pine Slope, but when I first started working here, when I was a freshman, we had a downpour that lasted like three days. You remember that?"

"No, not really. I mean, I was in middle school," said Robbie.

"Oh yeah," Chris laughed. "I forgot you're a baby. Well, anyway, on TV, they called it a superstorm; a large front just basically stopped over us. It rained for three or four days straight. Just like now. I think my parents said we are getting like two feet of rain or some shit. Anyway, all this dirt and mud up here eroded right down the slope. When I came to work the following week, some of the graves had completely washed away. Wooden caskets were exposed. A few of them had broken completely, and leather boots and leg bones were sticking out of the ground. Swear to God."

"What? You're joking," asked Robbie. "The dead people's legs were sticking out of the ground?"

"Femurs, tibias, human bones all over the place. The rain washed some of them right down the hill into the lake. So, I started calling this Bone Hill. The sickest thing was that there's an area of Pine Slope that's called Child Yard, you know why?"

"Kids' graves?" asked Robbie.

"Yep," said Chris proudly. "Most of this section and Maplewood, those are mostly adults. Oakwood, Shady Lawn, and Rest Haven are all veterans and old people. But this area was used only to bury dead kids. Mostly infants. If you look at the dates, most of 'em died before they were a year old. Probably TB or something. After that big rainstorm, I found the creepiest doll head. It was all smashed up and had flies all over it. I think it was from inside a baby's casket. Anyway, no one ever comes up here anymore. Just us workers, to mow and whack the weeds. That's it. Not another soul, ever. Too creepy."

"Wow," said Robbie.

"The only kids' graves that survived were the mausoleums up here, which are abandoned. They were the ones the earliest settlers built; they go back to the 1800s. But no one has opened them up since then. The families that own them are all gone, I think, or their descendants got buried somewhere else, I guess. So, while we still must mow around them, no one ever goes in them. Harold said the cemetery lost all the keys, so they don't even have a way to get inside. The doors are solid, like a bank vault. They're pretty much forgotten now. Until you found that key."

They walked up to a large, square granite building with the name *Amontillado* carved in granite over the front lintel. The door was copper and had turned green from generations of weathering. Robbie inserted the key into the lock, and it turned gracefully.

"It works," he yelled. The rain had started to come down even harder. "Get in here," he said to Chris, slowly swinging the two-ton door wide open and then closing it behind them. "I can't believe the hinges still work."

Chris walked in first and pulled off the hood of his poncho. Water streamed down onto the steps down to the dusty floor. The remnants of dried flowers were propped up in a vase on the stained-glass window, which had bars on the outside. A small marble altar with a carved cross on it stood underneath it. Because of the thick, stained glass and the metal bars, there was no way to see inside or out of the building.

"I've never been inside one of these. It's like a little church," said Chris.

"What'd you expect, cable TV?" Robbie laughed.

"I don't know; it's just an interesting building," said Chris, looking around. "It's actually in great condition. Probably hasn't been opened in a century. Look at the dates," Chris said, pointing to one of the sealed sarcophaguses. "This guy was born in 1818, died eighteen years later. That's not exactly a ripe old age but not a baby either."

"Look at their birthdates and dates of death," said Robbie. Each of the five tombs had birthdates and death dates exactly eighteen years to the date of their birth. "Is there anyone buried in here younger or older than that?"

"Doesn't look like it," said Chris. "Why'd they build this whole mausoleum for dead teenagers? Did they all die from the same disease?"

"Doubt it," said Robbie, stepping down toward the caskets. "They didn't die in the same eras. This guy, Frederick, died in the 1850s. This other guy died in 1912. I don't see any connection; other than the last name and the fact they were all eighteen. Look at this one; there's no name carved on it. It's blank."

"Yeah... I don't get it," said Chris. "I just noticed something else weird."

"What?" asked Robbie.

"I didn't notice it until now, but there was this fine dust on the floor leading up to that empty tomb over there. It had footsteps in it. Sneaker prints," said Chris. "Let me see the bottom of your sneakers."

"What?" asked Robbie.

"I said, let me see your shoes."

"Uh, ok," said Robbie, leaning on the sidewall and turning his sole up, so they could inspect it.

"What the hell...." said Chris, trailing off.

The sneaker soles were distinctive, with a repeating V logo embedded in the rubber.

"Look," Chris said, pointing at the dust across the little room. The V logo of Robbie's sneaker was imprinted in the dirt several times up to the empty tomb. It appeared someone wearing the same sneakers had entered the room previously and walked up to the open grave. "Robbie, have you been in here before? How did you get that key?"

"I told you, I have something nice for you to give Nicole. It's your eighteenth birthday today, isn't it, Chris?" Robbie asked, stepping closer to him. "I'll take care of giving it to Nicole now, don't worry," he said, bashing the right side of Chris' skull with a heavy crowbar that had been propped up inside the door.

"For the love of God, Robbie, what are you doing!?" he gurgled.

Robbie struck him two more times on the temple. Christopher lost consciousness and crumpled to the floor. Robbie smashed Chris' head several more times. Scarlet blood began to richly flow from Chris' head wounds and pool up on the marble floor. Robbie sopped it up with a cloth he had brought with him.

Robbie kicked Chris' limp body twice until it rolled into the tomb. He smashed his brain cavity several more times. Chris was dead.

Robbie slowly tugged a marble slab across the front of the tomb and pushed Chris' body deep inside. The stone locked neatly. He used the crowbar to ensure that there was a perfect fit. There was no way to know it hadn't been sealed up tight for a century.

He stood up, walked back up the steps to the outside of the mausoleum, and looked around. There were acres of cemetery between him and anyone else this early in the day, especially in the torrential rain. He turned back, locked, and secured the front door. It was impenetrable without the key and would probably remain sealed for another five generations.

The mud had already washed away their footprints leading up to the stone building. Making sure not to leave any others, Robbie took off his sneakers and walked back down to the golf cart parked at the bottom of the hill. He threw the crowbar, his sneakers, the bloody rag, and the key into a small duffel bag that was filled with heavy rocks. He zipped up the bag.

He drove the cart back to the maintenance shed. Before he did, he threw the heavy bag with the key, the bloody cloth, and his sneakers into the center of the deep lake. The bag containing the evidence of the crime quickly sank into the murky depths below. He had brought a new pair of sneakers in the bag that he had stashed in the maintenance shed.

"Robbie Montresor, have you seen Chris?" Harold asked when he arrived at work a little before noon. "Sorry I'm late; this weather was awful."

"No, he never showed up for work," said Robbie, drinking some coffee. "He never clocked in. I was here at seven. I assumed he overslept. Did you call him at home?"

"Yeah, his mother thought he had gone to work, but no one heard him leave. You haven't seen him?"

"Nope, not since Friday. I saw him at the movies with his girlfriend Nicole last week, that was it. I think they were celebrating his birthday. He probably got drunk and overslept."

"Ok, I'll let his mother know we haven't seen him and that he never clocked in," said Harold.

"I'll check with Nicole," said Robbie. "She might know where he is. She works at the mall; I think her shift starts at noon."

AMISH

By Sarah Putnam Ropes

In the early 2000s, I was a rebellious teenage girl living near Lancaster, Pennsylvania. I was in a phase where I had just gotten a bunch of tattoos and sported a mohawk with pink hair. My friends were even more alternative, wearing studded leather jackets with studs protruding from them. We were quite a sight at the mall.

My wild friends and I used to sneak out of our parents' houses and bring beer and pot to this old, abandoned, and dilapidated farmhouse that was about an hour's walk from the nearest road. Two of my friends had off-road four-wheelers with tow carts, so it took a lot less time for us to get there across the fields. On a good night, it only took us twenty minutes, but the ground was rugged and bumpy. A car wouldn't be able to make it there; it would take a Jeep or off-road vehicle.

Anyway, it was a great place that we could chill all night and not have to worry about cops or neighbors bugging us. Not once did a car drive anywhere nearby, where we could even see headlights.

We always climbed up to the top floor, as it had the least amount of debris and had a nice wide-open area where we could all just sit in a big circle and casually hang out. We could also look out the broken windows and see if anyone was approaching from any direction.

We always brought a few flashlights and battery-operated lanterns since we were far away from any other significant light sources. It was dead silent other than the crickets chirping and the sounds of our own laughter.

One night, it was a warm summer Saturday, and there were eight of us in the farmhouse. It was very late, about 3 a.m., and we had been hanging out for a couple of hours, just drinking and smoking. We were getting ready to leave soon and call it a night. There was some starlight and moonlight, but not much. We were feeling pretty chill.

Suddenly, we heard the front door downstairs creak open, and we heard some chatter. We quickly hid our booze and joints, sat as still as possible, and hoped no one came upstairs. We assumed it was the police and figured someone must have called them to bust us. But this was where things got weird.

An Amish family came trudging up the stairs into our room. The father was a gray-haired, bearded man in his early fifties, his plain-looking wife wore a white bonnet, and their three daughters were following right behind them. They were all dressed in black and white Amish-style clothing, that kind they wear that is out of the 1800s.

The parents were busy chatting to each other, but it wasn't in English. It might have been Dutch or maybe German, but I really can't say. Two of the little girls, about six or seven years old, were speaking to each other in English. The third girl didn't say anything.

They all walked up into the room and continued to talk to one another like we weren't there. It was as if they were looking through us instead of at us. At one point, one of the little girls was standing only a few feet in front of my face and said excitedly to her sisters, "This is going to be my room!"

The mother sat down and started knitting as though she had lived there forever.

We just sat there, frozen. We all looked at each other as if to say, 'Is this really happening?' but we didn't say a word.

The father and other girls in the Amish family continued to walk around and look at the room. They acted as though they were checking out a new house they were going to move into. But if you saw the state of this house, you'd know that was impossible. It was far beyond repair. It was also three in the morning, in the darkness, in the middle of nowhere.

Yet, this entire Amish family was walking around the building for at least ten minutes, talking and sitting down. They were oblivious to our presence. Again, there was no way they couldn't see us. The lanterns were all lit. The fact they didn't say anything about us, or to us, was jarring. Here we were, drinking and smoking, with pink mohawks and leather studded jackets, and yet, they didn't even make eye contact with any of us, much less say anything to us. They looked real, substantial, and not transparent.

They finally walked back down the stairs. We heard the front door open and shut and then silence. No vehicle driving away, no more voices, nothing. Just crickets again.

Several of us dashed downstairs to investigate. We brought three flashlights with us and ran out the front door. There was no one and nothing to see. No vehicles, no tire tracks in the gravel road, no Amish people, no footprints, nothing. Now keep in mind, this was only a minute or two after we heard the front door slam shut.

If they had been on foot, they wouldn't have made it very far. We would have seen or heard any type of vehicle, even a horse-drawn buggy. This was flat, open prairie grassland, and we could see for miles, even in the darkness. We never went back to that farmhouse.

17.

APPARITION

By Gulzaz Ahmadi

In 1991, my family had been living in a split-level ranch house in Hackensack, New Jersey. At the time, my father was 46 and a husky guy with jet black hair. My brother (who was about 15 at the time) and I were up late watching Saturday Night Live in our living room.

It was just after the show ended at about 1:00 a.m., and we had been laughing about the show loudly. We heard our parents' bedroom door open, and we both said to each other, "damn, we just woke Dad up." We looked over at the bedroom door, and it was now wide open, but we could hear our father snoring in bed.

Standing there in the open doorway was an old man. He was slightly hunched over, wearing a white buttoned-up dress shirt with a collar and blue dress pants. He had completely gray hair and looked straight at us. He was relatively thin, but he was completely solid, not transparent or anything like that.

After two or three seconds, he vanished. My brother and I instantaneously looked at each other and said, "Did you just see an old man?"

We then described to each other *exactly* what we had just seen, and it was identical. When we crept over to the bedroom to investigate, our father was still in bed, snoring. He had never gotten up. Our mother was next to him, sound asleep as well.

My brother and I have talked about this experience many times over the years since then and tried to figure out if we saw a ghost that night.

The weird thing is that now in 2021, exactly 30 years later, our father looks *identical* to the apparition that we saw in 1991. He looks gaunt and thin, has gray hair, and has the same posture (slightly hunched over) that he didn't have then, but which the apparition had. It was most certainly him in the future that we saw that night.

18

BEDROOM

By Zhi Huang

From when I was three to ten years old, my family lived in a tiny second-floor walkup apartment in a large city. Our apartment was long and narrow, and my family had to walk through my bedroom to get to the bathroom, so it was a cramped lifestyle, to say the least.

Around when I turned eight, my parents decided to offer me a wee bit of privacy, asking me if I wanted to move into a separate bedroom that had its own entrance/exit from the entry stairwell. It was extremely small, basically a closet, but I was eager to move in there because it was private and at least away from my parents and baby brothers.

From the very first night they moved my bed into this room, I saw a very dark shadowy presence fading in and out of the wall. It had no eyes but razor teeth. His mouth opened to silently scream.

I thought I was going crazy. I never told another soul about it. I saw it nearly every night for two years. He was tall and thin and a living shadow; that's all I can do to describe him.

The walls were plastered with children's animal-themed wallpaper from the previous owners. If I recall, it had strange little toy animals repeated over and over. Because of the bizarre events happening in that room, this innocent décor seemed ominous.

My mother would occasionally come into my room to check on me, and I would be soaked through my pajamas in my own sweat from hiding under the cheap blankets. I was petrified of that room. I was living in hell, but I had no options because my baby brothers now slept in my old room. I became sleep-deprived and unhealthy. I think my teachers might have commented on my deteriorating mental state to my parents. Thank God we eventually moved away.

It has been nearly forty years since we moved out of that horrible apartment. We moved many miles away to another province, and I have never been back since then.

Just last year, I decided to make the long trek to my old neighborhood with my boyfriend. He parked the car, and we were walking around when I ran into a familiar-looking elderly woman sweeping the sidewalk outside the building next door to my old apartment. I approached her and introduced myself.

Shockingly to me, she remembered both my parents and even remembered me from when I was a child. She told me that our old apartment had a tragedy in it... in my old bedroom. Decades ago, a young man in his early 20's killed himself in that room while his parents were away on vacation. The neighbors eventually smelled a terrible odor and called the police. They found his dead body in my old bed. Apparently, he left a suicide note in which he said that the shadows plagued him all night long and convinced him to take the pills.

HELL

By Joseph C. Gioconda

"**I**'m not like the rest of you," Sol said to Karen, stomping his cigarette out on the ground with his foot. They were hanging around outside the Grace Tabernacle Church in Portland as others milled about. "My experience was way different than yours."

They shuffled back into the building and sat down on rickety metal chairs in the stale church gymnasium. Two dozen people of all different walks of life settled in with cheap, cold coffee in Styrofoam cups in hand. Despite the drab surroundings, they looked forward to gathering once a month here. They all shared a unique experience that even their own family members couldn't understand.

"Ok, welcome back, everyone. We heard from Whitney right before the break," said Christy, the founder of the group who had her own near-death experience at twelve years old when she fell through the ice in her grandparents' pond.

"Sol, you've been coming to the group for almost two years now, and you've never shared anything. Are you ready to share this time?" she asked.

Sol straightened up in his seat. "I am ready."

The others shushed each other and listened intently. They had wondered about Sol's experience for a long time.

"Back in Tennessee as a kid, I was bad. I mean, *bad*. When I turned fourteen, I started stealing. My old man was a drunk and had left us when I was a baby. My mom was a waitress at a diner and was never home at night. So, my brothers and I, we got into a lot of trouble with the law. I did my share of petty larcenies until I was eighteen. Then, I graduated to Grand Theft Auto. More money in it. My fence introduced me to selling hard drugs. Narcotics were new back then, and there was a lot of money to made in it. A lot. I mean, I had more money than anyone my age. I was driving around in a Cadillac at sixteen. It was glorious. But it got worse."

He took a sip of the bad coffee and winced.

"I decided to rob a liquor store. I knew the owner, so he was shocked. He pulled out a shotgun on me, but before he could cock it, I fired my pistol straight into his face. He died instantly. Police never caught me. I went on to do more terrible things. I spent time in and out of prison until I was in my early thirties. I got married, got divorced, had a couple of kids that I abandoned. I was a real asshole."

"Sounds like it," a male member of the group piped up.

"I don't deny it," Sol continued. "I won't even tell you all the worst of it. Nine years ago, I decided to flee Tennessee, from some felony warrants. So, I was driving cross country, across the Rockies alone in a beat-up Chevy. It was snowy, and I guess I didn't appreciate how dangerous the roads were. An oncoming truck swerved toward me, and I lost control of my car. I skidded off an embankment at about sixty. Car dropped off the edge straight down and hit a tree. I felt myself die."

"Thank you. Can you elaborate a little on that last point, Sol?" asked Christy.

"My face crashed through the windshield. I felt my head crack open like a walnut. There was no mistaking it. The skull fracture was so bad, I felt my brain ooze out. Suddenly, I was outside the car, above it. Looking down. I saw my own head, my crumpled body, the crashed car. I saw steam coming out of the radiator. I was floating above. That's when I realized I had died. There was no pain; I just felt the sensation of floating weightlessly.

"I have heard the rest of you for the last two years describe your own Near-Death Experiences. They all sounded wonderful, and I am jealous. You described beautiful angels, beings of light, even having met Jesus Christ. You've described being drawn to a great light filled with love. Jeremy, I remember you saw your dead mother and father, and they welcomed you to a place of pure peace, isn't that what you said?"

"Yes, it changed my life forever, Sol. I have no fear of dying now," Jeremy said.

"Well, I didn't see what you all saw. I looked around, and everything went dark. I felt myself being drawn, like with a big vacuum, downward. Fast. Into a bottomless pit. An abyss. And it got wicked hot. Not like a summer day. Like a volcano. A lake of fire. I felt flesh rip off my ribcages. It wasn't my real flesh since my body was already dead, face down back in that car. It was my spiritual body, and it just kept tearing off. The pain didn't cease."

"What did you see, Sol?" asked Christy.

"Creatures that had the most horrific faces I have ever seen. They had nothing but hatred and contempt for me... for all of us. For humanity. They took delight in torturing us. They wanted nothing but more souls to satisfy their bloodlust. And there were thousands of them. Not just a few. Each had a twisted, distorted body. Some of them had things growing on their backs that were burned and blackened. They were blackened feathers, wings that were burnt. Others had gray gelatinous appendages. They were clawing and grasping at me. The sounds of their guttural moaning and indescribable stench of sulfur remain with me to this day."

He paused for a moment, shuddering, before continuing.

"Then I was pulled down further into a cold, dark, watery place.

When I reached the very bottom, it resembled the entrance to a cave, with what looked like spider webs hanging. I heard cries, wails, moans, and gnashing of teeth. I saw more beings that resembled humans, with the same shape of a head and body, but they were ugly and grotesque. They were frightening and sounded like they were being tormented, in agony.

"I also saw regular people. Humans like us. They were buried in deep dirty pits up to their necks, and the creatures were setting them on fire over and over. One of the people being tortured looked at me, and I recognized him. It was a guy I had once dealt drugs with named Vince. Vince died in a gunfight with a rival gang a while back. Vince looked at me and said to me, 'Sol, don't come back here. You must save yourself. There is no way out. No way out. Ever.'

"This scene was burned into my soul. It was like nothing I have ever seen before or since. I knew instantly that there was no escaping this place once you were sent here.

"I looked up and saw a light in the far distance, behind the creatures. It was just a dot but against the bleak darkness, it stood out. I looked at that tiny pinprick of light and made a promise to it. I said, 'if you give me one more chance, just one, I will repent and never sin again.' I was pulled upward back toward my body, and suddenly, I heard a voice say, 'you get only one more shot, Sol. Don't waste it.'"

HOPE

By Michael Sepulveda

"How are you feeling today, 231Q?" An elderly scientist dressed in a pristine white coat asked the younger, more sedated, and restrained boy.

He looked up groggily and spat in the scientist's face.

Unamused, the doctor wiped it away with his sleeve.

"Go... to hell." 231Q flexed his otherworldly muscles but with the number of drugs coursing through his system and the myriad of locks strapping him to his chair, he could not break free.

"Now now, 231Q. Let's be amicable here; we'll treat you with kindness and be gentle. All you need to do is cooperate. A fair trade, wouldn't you say considering what has happened, yes?" Mr. Covack said somewhat cheerfully.

"My name... is... Ben, you monster." Ben's eyes turned white.

Startled, Covack took a few steps back when he saw a portion of the room begin to distort and bend reality in an unnatural fashion. He pushed a button on the wall and spoke into the intercom.

"Pump him up, now!"

No vocal response was given, but Covack could see several streams of liquid snake their way into Ben's veins through IVs in both of his arms. Slowly but surely, the spatial distortion disappeared, and Covack relaxed enough to approach the battered young man again.

"Most experiments are failures due to human error; did you know that 23... Ben? I'm sure you of all people would know, you are a monument to that fact after all."

Covack waited for a response as normally the smallest amount of provocation would set Ben off, no matter how doped up he was. This was new. Covack took out a tape recorder and hit record.

"Note 398: subject 231Q appears to have his spirit broken, that, or we managed to hit the correct dosage to keep him under indefinitely. More experimentation with the drug cocktails is needed."

He paused the recorder and turned his attention back to Ben. It was then that Ben mumbled something under his breath.

"For... ever," Ben said, softly yet with a hint of rage on his lips.

"What was that? Talk to me; we are here to help you. Not hurt you, remember that." Covack implored.

"You... you don't want to help me! You want to keep me locked in this godforsaken place and poke and prod me, force me to do horrible experiments with my body! My spirit is not broken, doctor... you just made it so I can't distort reality, for now. You can't keep me down here forever."

Ben looked up at the frightened doctor with unfocused eyes and a knowing smile. The doctor's fear, however, was replaced by anger as he pulled out a pistol and fired multiple bullets at Ben's forehead.

The bullets landed on the ground harmlessly. Ben laughed weakly at this, and Covack threw the gun angrily at the wall behind him, his professionalism lost. A rather rare occurrence.

"Don't want to hurt me, huh, Doc? Hah... right." Ben chuckled to himself. "What kind of doctors and government lock up their own superhero? I saved... people! I saved, hah, the planet! And this is how I'm repaid?" Ben's eyes flickered white for a moment, but the constant stream of drugs prevented him from accessing his powers.

Covack ran up to the former hero and shouted in his face.

"You slaughtered hundreds of people! Created a puppet show with the corpses of those you murdered and induced madness with that unfathomable distortion ability! Thousands have died by your own hand!" Covack paused for a moment to compose himself and pulled away from the hero he used to idolize as a child. "Do you know what a god is when he cannot control his desires? A demon, Ben, a monstrous hellion deserving of death. But we can't kill you, not yet. But we will find a way, that I promise you."

"I knew it! You don't want to help me like I even want you to, but still, I'd much rather not be killed and toyed with like this. Hypocrites, the whole lot of you."

"We just want to know, Ben. We just want to know."

"Know... what?"

The drugs were starting to have a much stronger effect on him now, most likely due to the prolonged use of them. Covack knew that this might be his only chance to get a genuine answer from the man.

"You've been alive for... centuries, Ben. What over that period did you see that turned you... into this?"

This question seemed to make Ben somber, and he held his head low before looking up to Covack, completely lucid for once.

"I'm surprised it took you this long to ask."

"Yes, Ben, hurry before madness overcomes you again, don't let termination be the only choice left for you."

Ben nodded at this and continued.

"My last mission in space... when I stopped that asteroid, I was pulled into a small portal that even I could not detect. It was some kind of... ethereal dark dimension. At first, I thought I was alone and tried to use my distortion ability to tear a hole back home. But I was stopped by... *it.*"

"Ben, what did you see?"

"A behemoth of apocalyptic proportions, an amalgamation of the vilest creatures and monstrosities unimagined by humanity ever since our inception. I fought against it and its horde for... years, and by some luck, I managed to escape, but it left my mind shattered." Ben started laughing. "We're all going to burn! We're all going to die, aha! Yes, it shall come! It shall come!"

Covack rushed over to the intercom again.

"For God's sake, pour some more sedatives into him, now!" Covack ordered, and soon after, Ben returned to a more docile state.

The doctor left him, and the door sealed behind him. Another doctor came up to him and asked what to do after this revelation. Covack closed his eyes and bit his lip.

"We may have to free 231Q."

LURED

By Amy Yun Yu

"**T**he monster spread its tentacles wide, slithering over the walls as Anastasia stood frozen in the center of the room."

Nathan lowered his voice dramatically, noiselessly flipping the page of the storybook as he read it aloud. Clarice, his baby sister, had picked it up from the bookstore they'd stopped at on their way to the middle of nowhere.

"Slowly, tentacles crept towards her in the dark. The movement was no more than a whisper over the cold tiled floor. Anastasia shivered. They were close. She took in a breath and… WHAM!" He poked his sister, who shrieked and jumped off the bed. Her nostrils flared as she looked at him angrily.

"NATHAN!!!" Their mother shouted from the tiny kitchenette where she'd been banging pots for the last hour.

"JERK!" Clarice said though he could see amusement dancing over her face beneath her phony rage.

"I'm sorry. You picked a book not suitable for your age. What were you thinking?" Nathan tucked seven-year-old Clarice in her bed and pulled up the covers.

"I just liked the book. I felt as if it was calling out to me," she told him in a soft voice.

He smiled. "Keep it from mom, will you?"

Clarice nodded before she closed her eyes. Placing a kiss on her forehead, he forced himself to go to his mother. His head banged against the ceiling as he stood up. He cursed the low roof of their mobile home as he walked out of the room.

"We're in the middle of nowhere, and all you can think of is having fun with some screaming," his mother complained, trying to shove the frying pan in one of the drawers. It didn't fit. She tried slamming it close, but it cracked.

Without a word, Nathan took it away from his mother and guided her towards a small sitting area. He turned off the lights as he went.

"How could he do this to us?" His mother's shoulders shook as she fell on the settee by the window.

Nathan patted her shoulder awkwardly and looked outside, internally cursing his father and his debts.

They'd parked their trailer in a wide grassy field beside a lake. Dark mountains loomed at a distance. The wind whistled through the thick trees on the other side of a tiny road leading to God knows where. Fog snaked through the grassy fields, clinging onto dwarf grass blades. It was thick around their trailer, and Nathan knew that if he stepped outside, he wouldn't be able to see his feet.

"What's she doing out there?" His mother blurted out. "Clarice... Clary?" She called, her eyes on the glass.

Nathan followed her line of sight and felt his heart drop when he saw his sister standing there, motionless with her right hand gripping one of the long ears of her plush bunny. She was a dark figure against the white fog in the full moon.

"What the hell?" Nathan choked.

Without a moment of hesitation, his mother pushed him back and opened the trailer door. She rushed towards the lone figure she'd seen standing in the fog. When she rounded the corner, she skidded to a stop. Clarice wasn't there.

"Clarice!!!" She shouted, looking around hysterically. Her voice echoed in the empty expanse around her.

Clarrriceeee!

The wind howled in the night as if aiding her search for her daughter. She repressed a shudder and briskly walked towards the lake. Clarice had been standing beside it. What if she'd fallen in? She shook her head and quickened her steps.

The fog was thick over the lake. The water was eerily still. The wind picked up, pushing fog towards the dark of the trees.

Shoving her fear somewhere deep down, she took in a deep breath and dived in the lake. Clarice had to be there. She just knew that.

It was dark under the water than the world above. Everything was still. There was nothing to hint at Clarice's presence. Maybe she went back to the trailer? She thought and swam towards the surface. The moment her face broke the surface, something snaked around her ankle, pulling her back. Water covered her head before she could scream. She had just enough breath to look down at something dark clinging to her leg. A hand? No, a tentacle.

It slowly crept up her body, razor-sharp teeth puncturing her skin as it went. She opened her mouth to scream, but water rushed in, choking her. Then, finally, the thick fog parted, and moonlight shone over the lake's surface. Against that light, smoky tentacles scattered throughout the lake.

The moment that his mother had rushed outside, Nathan had run towards the room. He'd tucked Clarice in only a moment ago, and he refused to believe that she would've climbed out of the window during the night.

Sure enough, she was sitting up in her bed with her eyes wide.

"You're..." Nathan couldn't form a word. Goosebumps spread through his body.

"It's coming," Clarice whispered.

"What's coming? Why aren't you asleep? Did you step out?"

She shook her head, pulling her bunny close. Then, before Nathan could ask her more, he noticed that wind had stopped howling, and it was pin-drop silent out there. He couldn't hear their mother calling for Clarice. Where had she gone?

Swallowing, he walked towards the window. It was so dark; the fog was a dark abyss over the field in the full moonlight. He gasped and rubbed his eyes. He was seeing things. Surely there couldn't be a black fog. But, no, it was still there.

Behind him, he heard the rustling of the sheets as Clarice got down off the bed. Her tiny feet patted on the cold trailer floor as she joined him.

"It's coming," she repeated.

Nathan jumped with a start when the storybook fell from the small bedside table. The sound echoed throughout the trailer. He stilled, and everything around him felt like it was holding its breath.

As he bent down to pick up the book, he found shadowy tentacles climbing up their mobile home.

Animal fear gripped Nathan, rendering him motionless. He could only watch as they covered up the trailer, cutting off soft moonlight's glow that filtered in through the windows.

He scooped up Clarice in his arms and dove for the light switch. He turned on all the lights as he ran for the sitting area. There, a window had been left open. He could see dark tentacles moving in. He slammed the window closed, cutting them off. He watched, with his eyes wide and heart thundering in his chest, as the tentacles dissolved into nothingness.

He staggered back a step and pressed himself against the wall. He raked his hands through his hair, pulling at them as he forced himself to believe that what he was seeing wasn't a dream.

"It's from the storybook," Clarice whispered, from where she was curled up in the corner of the settee.

He wanted to shake her, to make her believe that such things didn't happen.

There was no way out of the trailer now. That thing had it all covered. Pushing his fear back, Nathan straightened up. He had to get his sister out of here no matter what.

"Storybook?" he asked.

"Yes…" Clarice said.

Nathan had tons of questions, but he decided to believe Clarice.

"Stay here. I'll be right back," he told her and retraced his steps back to the room. He had to get that storybook. He had to know what they were dealing with.

Lights winked when he was at the threshold. He stopped, looking around for anything dark. So far, so good. The book was just there, lying on the floor, and opened to the page he'd been reading. For some reason, the room was cold. He could see his breath cloud in front of him.

Tentatively, he started for the book. A dark swimming mass of fog stilled at his movements outside the window. For a moment, the only sound he could hear was his heart beating in terror and his sister sobbing in the living room. It was now or never.

The moment he dove for the book, the trailer shook, followed by an ear-piercing animal-like growl.

BAM!!! Something heavy landed on the trailer's roof, causing a dent to appear right over Nathan's head. That was the moment when the lights went out and the window to his left shattered. Somehow, the book was still a few feet away from his reach.

A distinctive hum overtook the silence of the night, causing the trailer to vibrate. Things fell from the shelves, pots clanged in the kitchenette, and Clarice screamed.

Nathan mistakenly looked up at the broken window, where the fog had cleared up a bit to let the moonlight in. And in that light, he saw something he'd never forget. A creature in the dark with eyes as red as blood and mouth open wide like a Cheshire cat's. Rows of sharp pointed teeth looked down at him, blood dripping from them.

Despite himself, he screamed and jumped back. He ignored the book as he hurled everything between himself and the monster. Scented candles fell onto the bed, fire catching the bedspread and then the curtains. As Nathan ran out of the room, he turned his head just in time to see the monster flinch just a little in the growing fire.

"Get up, Clary. Quickly!" He yelled to his sister, reaching for the candles his mother had stocked in the kitchenette cabinet. She loved having candles burning around the house, and when they'd left in a hurry, he'd argued with her for bringing them. Now he was glad that his mother hadn't listened to him.

With his hands shaking, he started lighting them up one by one.

"Hurry!" Clarice whispered urgently, her eyes on the bedroom where the tentacles had started making their way from between the fire. The monster hovered just outside the window, its eyes on them. What was it waiting for?

He heard a loud thump on the roof again. Nathan dropped a candle with a start. The sound was followed by a scratching sound as if something was dragging its claws down the surface. As if aiming to tear open the roof.

Swallowing, Nathan peeked at the monster. It was nowhere in sight.

"Up there." He looked at Clary and then at the roof above them. Claws had pierced the thick metal roof, and all he could see beyond it was darkness. And a single red eye peering down at them.

Clarice screamed, losing it entirely.

"Clarice, please!" He begged, sobbing as he worked on lighting all the candles. He'd managed to light only seven of them. He looked around their mobile home one last time and kicked open the main door.

He was met with thick dark fog. Before the tentacles forming in the fog could enter, he pulled down the curtain and set it on fire. He kicked it out the door before fire could catch up to the rest of the things inside and trapping them.

A burning piece of cloth pushed back the darkness. Taking advantage of it, Nathan pulled down more curtains and anything he could get his hands on. He set them all on fire and hurled them out of the trailer park, clearing a way for them in the fog.

The moment he saw an opening to the bright field beyond, he scooped wailing Clarice in his arms. He closed his eyes, ignoring the sound of the monster shrieking and of tentacles slamming into the trailer to turn it upside down. He ignored the feeling of something slithering on the floor behind him, of it traveling up his leg. He felt the sharp needles poke into his skin, drawing blood, but he stood straight for Clarice.

"Listen to me, Clary," he whispered in his sister's ear. She was sobbing and trembling violently in his arms. "You're gonna run, and you're gonna run fast. You won't stop, and you won't look back. Travel back the way we came from, get help but don't come back."

Clarice tried to protest, but he pressed her close, shushing her. Then, the moment she nodded, he jumped out the door.

The monster quieted, and all the sounds faded away. But tentacles held onto him. It was as if the monster was letting him loose only to pull him back. Behind him, the trailer burned. An inferno on a dark, cold night.

Just when Nathan felt that the monster was about to pull him, he let Clary on the ground. She was shaking but had stopped crying.

"Go," he whispered, tears sliding down his cheek.

Clarice threw her arms around him, squeezing him as violent sobs shook her. Then, she was gone, and Nathan suddenly felt icy cold.

Clarice running away on the dark lonely road was the last thing he saw before he was pulled back. He watched his sister as he was hurled up in the air towards the monster's gaping mouth.

A different sort of dread filled him up when he saw his sister stop and turn around to look. Her eyes were bright red, as the monster's. And in her hands, she carried the book. When she smiled, Nathan knew it was over.

All the pieces fell into place. They had lost the real Clarice back in that bookshop. The monster had donned the face of his sister and followed them back to where it could unleash itself. It'd devoured what it could, and now, Nathan had unleashed it to the world. It was just beginning. He'd seen the promise in the eyes of who he thought had been his sister.

MOUNTAINS

By Grace Elizabeth

H is hair, once fine and chestnut, was now aged mahogany. Strands of caramel ran wildly through his thick and lustrous locks. He had always been a relatively tall child, but as he aged, he only became taller.

Somehow, he wasn't spindly; there was bulk on him too, broad muscles beneath his crimson cotton shirt. His eyes held a mischievous glint that seemed to reflect the corners of his mouth, which always seemed to be fighting a smile. His eyes were every shade of brown you could imagine, a raw umber and caramel mix, dotted with bits of dark chocolate—much like the forest which surrounded his home.

They glowed with humour and playfulness that sent shivers down the spine and wrapped you in a warm embrace simultaneously. His hands, once smooth and soft, were calloused and tough, but they were his pride and joy. They told tales of his time in nature; of the work he had done to help others. They were the hands of one who had worked hard through every season; years of harsh sun had kissed the man's skin with golden hues that stretched over the light muscles in his face. A feather-light dusting of freckles darkened the bridge of his nose and gave a childish charm to his otherwise flawless skin. As he looked in the mirror, he smiled.

Ricky was only a boy when he made the decision to move to the mountains and start a new life. He had been in the bustling city for years, and he hated every honk of a horn, every taxi, every streetlight. He had always felt out of place in such a busy environment. He craved solitude and isolation and didn't want anything less than that. His father had died when he was fifteen, and instantly, he had been given the family fortune. He was heir to the Hawthorne legacy, so he didn't decline when the bank statement came through in his name.

The moment he hit eighteen, he bought a small home in the mountains. He had been looking at pictures online for years, but nobody had ever bought the rundown and ancient cabin. His father used to bring him to the mountains.

He began moving his belongings as soon as possible. His mother was sad to see him go, but she understood that he would never be happy if she tied him down to the city.

A few months later, he was walking through empty forests and spending his days reading novels in front of the fire. He had been close to his father. Losing him was more of a blow than he could have ever anticipated. It was a car accident. He hadn't been told the details, and to be quite honest, he didn't want to know them.

He lived alone for a few years, but when his mother got sick, she moved in with him into the cabin. She couldn't walk on her own but didn't tend to leave the house often, so she wasn't too much of a burden. Ricky had built a ramp leading from the deck of the cabin onto the path leading away from his home so she could use her wheelchair easily if there was an emergency.

As he sat on his sofa, he stared at the novel in front of him—reading but not taking the words in, not letting them seep into his brain like he normally would. He was distracted. Something felt eerily strange about the air. The sun was setting, and he thought it might be a good evening for a walk.

He went to grab the hunter's knife, which he left in the pouch but couldn't find it. The sun had barely set, but there was still an icy chill to the air biting him like a feral animal. He and his mother had been alone on the mountains for the entire duration of his stay, and that wouldn't change. He had inherited enough money to buy his home and all the land around it—so that was exactly what he had done. Nobody could get in; his land was impenetrable.

At least, that was what he thought before he saw the mutilated corpse on the floor.

It was turning the pristine white snow an ugly red. It was fresh, fresh enough that the red hadn't turned to a dingy brown colour, but rather it was bright against the pure ground. He reached out hesitantly and laid a trembling hand on the dead man's shoulder, pulling him onto his back so he could look at who was lying dead in the forest beside his home.

His breath hitched in his throat as he stared at the face of one of the security guards who scanned the perimeter of his land. Ricky shuddered; he felt a chill run down his spine, but it wasn't from the cold—he felt as if he was being watched, as if there was someone or something lurking deep in the forest. He stood, nearly collapsing at the sight of the bloody body in front of him.

He felt his eyes readjust—he had been focusing on this one part of the forest since he saw the corpse on the ground, but his breath started coming quick and fast as he realised there were more bodies scattered over the forest floor. Every guard he had hired was left on the snow like pieces of litter—discarded and still. Ricky wasn't sure where the strangled sob that left his throat came from or when his legs started moving. Before he could process what was going on, he was sprinting toward his cabin, glancing behind him at every opportunity: The blood-stained snow was still fresh in his mind. He twisted the handle on his door but found it already unlocked.

A hundred thoughts seemed to rush through his mind as his eyes darted from side to side, desperately trying to decide what to do. Nobody could have gotten up here without a vehicle, the climb was too steep, and in the icy conditions that had swept over the mountains like a plague—it would be too treacherous.

Ricky trekked around the side of his house; the snow was falling more now. The snow in which he stepped in became deeper with each fleeting second. He searched the outskirts of his house for a car or a snowmobile but found nothing. Suddenly, his mind flashed to his mother. There was a chance she had opened the door... at least that was what he told himself.

He wandered into the house and into the cabin, the smell of cinnamon hit him almost instantly. His mother insisted that burning them kept evil away from their home. Now, he was terrified that it had done the complete opposite. He jogged into the kitchen and picked up the phone to dial 911, he was shocked at how light it felt in his hands, and as he looked down, he figured out why.

The phone cord had been cut.

"Mum?" Ricky yelled, his voice cracked as he shouted, if anything had happened to her, he wasn't sure what he would do. He ran into her room, panting like a rabid dog as he pushed open her door.

Nothing.

He darted into the kitchen.

Nothing.

The bathroom.

Nothing.

Then he ran into his bedroom; he halted in the doorway—a flood of relief washed over him... she was sitting in her wheelchair facing away from him and reading one of the books he had left on his bedside table.

"Mum, what are you doing in here?"

She didn't answer.

"Listen, something has happened on the mountain; I need to use your phone and…"

Ricky stopped speaking when he realised she wasn't reacting to his words, she wasn't looking his way, her shoulders weren't moving up and down with breath, she was completely still.

Ricky forced himself to move forward, to put one foot in front of the other despite the fear that pumped through his veins like it had replaced the blood that once flowed there. He looked down at the pages of the novel, which were stained red with blood, blood that was still dripping from his mother's open mouth. Her eyes were wide open, bloodshot, and swollen like she had come face to face with the devil himself.

A hunter's knife was buried deep in her stomach. Blood fell from her mouth in a steady stream. He looked away, clasping a hand over his mouth, his lips quivering with every shaky breath he took. He dared one more glance back at his mother and realised that something was scrawled messily on the blood-stained pages of the book—he could barely make it out but squinted, nonetheless.

Hello, son.

He felt his heart halt in his chest; it wasn't possible—this was a psychopathic, cruel joke. He needed to find a phone, and he needed to find it quickly. He hadn't brought one with him because he thought it would disconnect him from a life in the mountains; that was a choice he sorely regretted.

He wanted to collapse to the floor, break down, and wait for the killer to find him—but there was still a chance of him escaping, finding a way through this maze of murder and bloodshed. He couldn't stay in the house; there was less of a chance of the killer finding him if he ran. He had to leave his mother behind, and as much as it hurt him to leave her body there for the animals of the forest, he didn't have a choice.

He hurriedly packed some canned fruit and bottles of water into a blue backpack, noting the creaks of floorboards around the house. The noises of one's house don't scare you until you feel like there is an intruder. Then every ordinary squeak and bang is a footstep or a knock; every blow of wind is a whisper.

He tried to block out the noises and move as quickly as possible, but his shaking hands betrayed him. He could survive without food for a while; he grabbed a jacket and ran out the door. The snow was falling heavily now; he could barely see ahead of him—the flurry of snow made it seem like everything around him was white. He ran deeper into the forest; his laboured breath was coming fast and hard. He stumbled and let out a small yelp as his hand landed in something warm and sticky. He brought it up so he could see it better and realised it was blood—he had fallen over one of the bodies from earlier.

He let out a cry of fear and sadness as the realisation that his mother was dead hit him like a wave crashing to the shore. He kept running until he reached the edge of the mountain. Earlier in the day, he could have scaled the cliff easily. He had taken rock climbing lessons numerous times as a child, but in these conditions, he couldn't see anything, and there was no telling just how slippery the surface of the rocks would be. He took a deep breath and turned to scale the mountain before him but felt a sharp pang of pain in his stomach. Strong hands gripped the handle of the blood-coated hunters' knife that had buried itself in his stomach. As he looked upwards, he saw his father's face—sneering and scarred.

Ricky felt his heart fall into a dark abyss as he let the life drain out of him.

FOLLOWED

By Joseph C. Gioconda

I think something followed me home from my vacation.

I recently got back from a weeklong trip, and the same activity from the old house I was staying in is now going on at my apartment. I apologize in advance for any incoherence in what I say because I haven't gotten much sleep the last several weeks, and I don't feel very well physically or mentally.

The house that we had stayed in was gorgeous, and since my entire extended family was staying there (eighteen people), it was also massive. It was split into two parts, the very old side of the house from the late 1700s (roughly just a basement studio and two bedrooms upstairs) and the newer side. I'm not going to go into much detail about the newer side as no paranormal activity took place there, but it was a gorgeous house. It cost my family a lot of money to rent during the summertime. It was apparently an old farmhouse.

I shared a room with my girlfriend Giselle, and since we were the last to arrive, we got the worst room in the house. Not only did we get the smallest room in the house (it was about ten feet by ten feet), but it was also on the old side of the house, directly in front of the basement stairs. As I had been driving for six hours that day, I was tired, so I said hello to everyone and quickly got into bed to go to sleep. However, from the drive and too much coffee, I was wired.

It was around 11 p.m. when Giselle and I got into bed. She's lucky in the sense that she can fall asleep just about anywhere in five minutes, so she was asleep within seconds. I had a weird uneasy feeling in my chest, not necessarily a scary feeling, just that annoying alert feeling you get when you feel like something is watching you. Plus, too much caffeine and six hours of driving didn't help relax my brain.

To help ease myself into sleep, I grabbed my iPad and hopped right down into a YouTube rabbit hole, jumping from video to video. I figured the mindlessness would get me to tire out and fall asleep.

About an hour into my journey online, I could tell that Giselle was having a nightmare, so I put my hand on her arm to gently wake her up, but as soon as I touched her, she bolted awake screaming, mumbled "the ghost" and immediately went back to sleep. I had just started to get tired, and safe to say I was sufficiently creeped out at this point, so back down the YouTube rabbit hole I went.

About another hour went by when she woke up screaming again, saying "the footsteps are close," and passed back out immediately. I decided I was apparently not going to sleep that night and went right back to YouTube. Yet another hour passed, and I saw her sit up in bed, but she was still asleep. She moved, so she was sitting on the edge of the bed and started having a conversation with the corner of the room. Her eyes were closed.

She eventually laid back down but not before I was terrified. I could have sworn I saw something like a shadow that was darker than the darkness of the room slide across the wall. The black figure seemed to appear in the corner where she was "staring" with her eyes closed. After I rubbed my bleary eyes, I concluded it was a mirage from staring at my iPad screen for too long.

Weird activity died down after the first night, usually just creaks in the floor or knocks on the wall/door. The only other standout event besides movement around the room happened on the second to last night when something sat down on the edge of my bed.

My first thought was that a cat had jumped on the bed, but I remembered I wasn't at my apartment, and my cat wasn't with us on vacation. I sat up just in time to see the indentation lift off the edge of the mattress. It couldn't have been my girlfriend as she was sleeping on the opposite side of the bed and nowhere near where the indentation happened. Also, the bed was as firm as a rock, so it was challenging to push that far down into it. It would have taken a very heavy person, not a housecat.

Fast forward one more sleepless night, and we were on our way home. After a long day of driving, we got back, and I settled down to watch some Netflix. My girlfriend had plans to go hang out with her friends, so she was out for most of the night.

I thought I'd finally get a break from the spooky stuff when my dog and cat both started tracking something around my apartment with their eyes. The way their heads were moving, whatever they saw was moving fast. Now I've seen them track bugs before, but neither of them really focuses on it too much, they usually just huff and ignore it, but this was different. Chip (my dog) started growling when whatever it was moved into the corner of the room. My cat Ava jumped up right next to me on the couch while Chip growled at the corner and started to slowly back up towards me.

After a full week of crap like this, I wasn't even scared anymore, just pissed off and tired because it likes to keep me from falling asleep. Chip and Ava both tracked the thing moving out of the corner towards us, so she started barking like crazy. After I got him to stop barking, I heard a growl come from the center of the room. It was high-pitched, like a small dog or a girl. Judging by where my pets were tracking, it looked like it was very short, very fast, and could jump up on the table and counters.

I stood up, stared in its general direction, and said, "Please leave."

I got a huge wave of chills and goosebumps in places I didn't know I could get goosebumps, but I said it again, much louder and sterner this time, while opening my front door to let it out. Whatever it was got really upset, it didn't do anything, but I could feel a lot of anger in the room. My pets tracked it moving towards the door, so I thought I was in the clear.

About two minutes later, Chip started barking at the corner of the room where the door was while my cat was on full alert staring at the same place. At this point, I just gave up and hoped it would leave me alone since it hadn't been violent yet, just annoying. Chip eventually fell asleep at my feet, and Ava had run into the other room, occasionally poking her head out the door to look in and immediately spring back into the room.

I just gave up on dealing with it at this point. I put my earbuds in to block out the knocks on the walls and watched television. I decided to stay up until my girlfriend got back home to let her know what was happening, but whatever it was took this as an opportunity to mess with me.

I was lying on my couch and kept feeling something poking me every five minutes. Not hard, just constant pokes on my arms and legs and feet. After this went on for a while, it pulled up on my nostrils. Again, I just ignored it because I learned it just got worse if I engaged with it. Whenever something like this would happen, I could feel the apartment get much colder, despite my thermostat saying it was seventy-two degrees. It felt like a meat locker.

After hours of knocking, poking, pulling, and the occasional arm brush from this... thing, my girlfriend finally got home. The second she got through the door, I could tell whatever it was left as I had no uneasy feeling, and there were no more weird noises, so I had one of the most restful nights I've had in over a week.

I don't know if it's gone for good or if it will come back tonight. Other than the growl and the short but overwhelming sense of anger, it hasn't been violent or disturbing, just annoying.

It has only been a couple of days since I wrote the first part of my story, but activity has been even higher since then. My girlfriend is seeing it now, and it is starting to get more aggressive. I also don't feel so good. For starters, I am running a fever out of the blue. My temperature was at 98.8 this morning (I checked because I had a fever the previous night), and it has risen again to 101.3 in only fifteen minutes. On top of these, the knocking and rustling noises around the apartment are now constant, and we hear dreadful laughing.

I feel drained; it's even hard to keep my eyes open despite a good night's rest.

Something is happening to me. The laughing I hear is non-stop, but I can't tell if it's in my head or real. I can't find Giselle or my pets. I swear it looks like things are moving around my apartment by themselves.

I need to sleep.

Ifinish story fever is 105 I cant barely see screen I cannot tell what is doing to me if Ican'twrite any more updatesit has won goodby

LOST

By Joseph C. Gioconda

Phil and Mike napped in the rental car. They were both awakened by the sound of gravel under the tires.

"Lou, what's up?" Mike asked, rubbing his bleary eyes. The clock on the dashboard said it was 3:35 a.m.

"I don't know," Lou replied in a strangely monotone voice.

"Huh?" Phil said. "Wait a minute... that road sign we just passed says we're in... Shiprock?"

Lou and Phil had decided to join their friend Mike on a long road trip from San Diego to the Grand Canyon. The 550-mile ride could take up to 10 hours each way. Phil was visiting from New Haven, so he had rented a mid-sized car which could easily accommodate their gear.

Initially, they thought they'd camp overnight along the way, but they decided to split the cost of a few nights at cheap motels instead. There were plenty on Route 8, which spanned from the coast to Routes 19, 10 and 17 in Arizona, which would take them north up to the Grand Canyon.

When they set out from the west coast in the late afternoon, it was mild and breezy. By the time they had reached El Centro, it was evening, but it was still over ninety degrees outside with no breeze. They found a cheap motel with air conditioning and spent the night.

The next day, after they slept late, they decided to make some progress toward their destination. They stopped in Yuma for lunch and crossed over into Arizona. Instead of stopping for another night in a motel, they decided to keep pressing forward and reach the Grand Canyon by morning.

Lou had been doing all the driving up until that point and offered to keep going straight through the night. By their rough calculations, they'd get to the edge of the Grand Canyon around dawn. They figured they would then check into a nice lodge, take a nap, and enjoy the rest of the day.

"Did you miss a turnoff?" Mike asked. "You should have turned off from Route 8 in Arizona, to go north. Shiprock, *New Mexico?* That's impossible. That's like 600 miles out of the way. And what road are we on?"

"Their road," said Lou, still driving.

"What the fuck is going on," asked Mike. "Lou, we let you drive for a few hours, and we're half a state out of the way?"

"They told me to come here," said Lou.

"Who? What the hell are you talking about?" asked Phil, equally growing frustrated with the driver.

"I was in Arizona," whispered Lou. "It was around midnight; I remember that. The highway seemed to stretch on forever in the dark. There were no lights ahead. Suddenly, I saw this flashing, blinking light. I couldn't tell if it was on the horizon or in the sky. So, I stopped the car and turned around, and it was on the other horizon too. So, I stayed put for a while. Eventually, the two lights seemed to come over us and merged. I must have fallen asleep by the side of the road. When I woke up, I remember that I was driving again, and we were here, on this gravel road. I'm really confused...."

"You're confused?" asked Phil sarcastically. "You probably fell asleep at the wheel and then somehow drove us hundreds of miles out of the way, and you're confused? Were you drinking?"

"Only coffee," said Lou. "Do you want to check my cup? You don't believe me?"

"Look, whatever happened," Mike said, "we gotta get back on the right road. Otherwise, we're going to end up screwing up the whole weekend. I need to get back to work in San Diego by Tuesday. If we spend another day driving around, we'll have zero time at the Canyon."

"Fine, Mike, you drive," Lou said, unbuckling his seatbelt and getting out of the driver's side door.

"No problem," Mike said, walking around the car and easing into the driver's seat. "Now, let's first find a diner or gas station. I desperately need coffee if I'm driving a few hundred miles."

"Ok, I looked on the road map and don't see anything around us," said Phil.

"All right, well, let's get back on the right road and see if we stumble on something." Even a crappy gas station would have coffee, Mike figured.

After an hour, they hadn't seen a single motorist passing in either direction. Suddenly, in the distance on the right, Mike saw a building. Above it was an old-style sign lit up in neon that said, "Diner Forever Open."

It was in mint condition. It looked like it had just been built as the chrome and steel of the exterior was shiny and perfectly undented. There weren't any cars parked outside in the parking lot. That seemed strange because a 24-hour diner would presumably have workers who drove there for their shifts; unless it wasn't really a 24-hour diner, and it was closed.

The sun was still an hour away from breaking in the east, and the sky had that strange pre-dawn glow to it. He woke up Phil and Lou and told them he had found a place to stop, use the restroom, and grab some coffee for the road.

"Where are we?" asked Lou.

"All night diner. Let's go, fellas," Mike said, getting out of the car and stretching my legs.

"Weird looking place," said Lou.

"Yeah," agreed Phil. "Strange vibe. But your driving brought us here."

They walked up the front stairs and through the front glass door. Even though not a single car was parked outside, the diner was completely full of people. Dozens of patrons sat quietly eating breakfast and drinking coffee. It was bizarrely quiet for being so crowded. Normally, a crowded restaurant would buzz with conversation. Instead, all they could hear was the clinking of the utensils against the plates. No one was saying a word.

"Table for three?" a waitress with perfectly coiffured red hair asked the boys, holding menus.

"Yes, thank you," Mike muttered.

"You're a long way from home now," she said.

"What? What do you mean?" he asked.

"Your license plate, California," she said, pointing outside.

"Yeah, we know," said Phil, clearly still annoyed with Lou's driving skills. "We're supposed to be—"

"—at the Grand Canyon?" the waitress interrupted.

"Uh, yeah, how did you know?" asked Phil.

"All these people were headed there," she said, gesturing to the silent but crowded restaurant.

"Wait, aren't we like hundreds of miles in the wrong direction?" Mike asked.

"Yes," she said.

"And where are all their cars?" asked Phil.

"They don't need them," she said, smiling. "And you won't need yours anymore, either. Come, have a seat."

DESPAIR

By Joseph C. Gioconda

Santiago was staying at a century-old seminary on the ocean for a summer retreat. Even though he didn't consider himself Catholic anymore, he had read that the four-day program was a nice way to get out of Los Angeles and spend some time in mostly silent contemplation. His latest girlfriend had dumped him, and he found it necessary to carve out some solitude.

He had never really prayed much. As a kid, his mother was Catholic and superstitious, but his father was essentially agnostic, so he barely learned how to pray. But when his friend Jacinto had intentionally overdosed on heroin last year, he started contemplating mortality. He had visited the parish church, and a very nice priest introduced himself.

Santiago explained to him that he was unaccustomed to these questions. Jacinto was a young man, barely twenty-three years old, when he took his own life. Where was he now? Heaven? Hell? He wanted to spend some more time thinking about these weighty questions.

The Gothic building on the coast once housed over a hundred men studying to become Roman Catholic priests. In recent decades, as interest in vocations dropped off, less than a dozen men lived in the building at any given time, and several of those were laypersons who managed the building and 300-acre grounds. The unspoiled waterfront property was invaluable, but the Church had been forced to sell off a few acres here and there to real estate developers to pay off unfortunate legal settlements.

Despite the extraordinary views of the Pacific, the bedrooms were sparsely furnished, and each had only a writing desk, dresser, sitting chair and closet. Bathrooms were shared at the end of the hall. The austere accommodations and incredible coastal views encouraged introspection for men considering their lifelong vocations and vows of poverty, obedience, and chastity.

The building had four floors, radiating like spokes on a wheel around a central staircase hub. Most of the wings were completely closed off to save on heating in the winter and cooling in the summer. During these retreats, they only used the first floor's eastern wing for temporary housing, a branch of the building which had less than a dozen rooms on either side of the hallway.

That first night, Santiago couldn't sleep. He tossed and turned in bed and stared at the old fan that wobbled on the high ceiling. Only a little light streamed in from the rectangular window above the door. A few sodium nightlights dotting the halls, giving the walls a sickly pale-yellow glow.

Suddenly, the distinct sound of a wooden chair falling over echoed throughout the hallways from upstairs. Santiago assumed someone must be bunking in the room directly above him, but he could have sworn the caretaker had mentioned everyone was accounted for on the first floor.

He also wondered why someone would be violently knocking over a heavy wooden chair at three o'clock in the morning. Did someone fall over after falling asleep in it? That accident would probably have made a greater racket, and if so, the person would have probably suffered a serious injury. But hearing nothing further, he went back to sleep.

The second day, Santiago attended Mass and a presentation by a

Capuchin monk who spoke about the afterlife. The monk described how souls ended up either with the beatific vision of God in heaven forever, stuck in Purgatory, or in a hellish torment forever. The monk also described the Catholic doctrine of limbo, where unbaptized infants supposedly reside. Finally, he described how the Church taught that anyone who took their own life was damned for eternity. Only God, the Creator of all life, was entitled to end one. If someone in abject despair were to commit suicide, God would be merciless.

Santiago didn't buy any of it. It sounded a lot like his mother. Like his father, he used to believe that when you died, you died. He also believed that in the highly unlikely event there was a Supreme Being who judged souls (as these people evidently believed), there was no way that He would let someone suffering so badly that they took their own life suffer even further in eternity. Such a being would presumably be merciful, not cruel and heartless. He thought about Jacinto and his reason for coming here, to this place.

The next night, Santiago was shaken awake by the thunderous echo of a wooden chair falling over upstairs again. He thought it was extremely odd and couldn't fall back asleep.

The next morning after dawn, during breakfast at the refectory, he walked over to the Capuchin monk, who was pouring a drink of orange juice from a pitcher into a glass.

"Good morning, Father," he said quietly.

"Hello, good morning," the elderly monk said with a smile.

"Can I ask you a quick question?"

"Of course," the monk said, sipping the orange juice.

"For the last two nights, at exactly three in the morning, I keep hearing a wooden chair fall over upstairs. It either falls or is violently thrown, but it's pretty loud. Last night, it woke me up and kept me up all night. Who's staying in the room above mine, so I can ask them to stop?"

"What room are you staying in?"

"On the first floor in the East wing, Room 7."

The monk suddenly looked pale and put the orange juice down.

"Do you want to change rooms?" he asked Santiago. "That shouldn't be a problem. One thing we have here are empty rooms."

"Uh, the room is fine. It's just that noise right above me. I thought no one was staying on the second floor."

"No one is," the monk said.

"I don't understand."

The monk sighed. "Back in the sixties, my friend Tommy Morrison was a great student, destined to be a great priest. But his parents didn't want him to get ordained. They wanted him to get married and have children since he was their only son."

"I still don't understand, Father," Santiago said.

"Tommy hanged himself in the middle of the night in Room 27. He kicked over the chair and dangled from the sprinkler pipe. We hear him crying every night in the chapel. Every night, he hangs himself again. I believe Tommy is damned, and this is his personal hell. Please pray for the souls in Purgatory. They may still be able to escape hell and reach heaven. But those who die by their own hand will wander the earth forever."

DARKWEB

By Joseph C. Gioconda

"Why is there blood on it?"

"It's obviously a hoax," said Brandon, peeling open the box's flaps to peer deeper inside. "So far, I found a bloody blouse, an ice pick and some news clippings. There's some other stuff at the bottom too."

"Shouldn't you be wearing gloves?" Drew asked nervously.

"Nah, I told you, this is all fake. I saw it before on YouTube," Brandon said dismissively.

"How much did you pay for this box?"

"Five hundred," said Brandon.

"You gave him your address? To send it to you?"

"Yeah, I had to."

"You should have used a post office box or something."

"Like I said, this stuff is bogus," said Brandon. "Now, be quiet; I have to broadcast this live. To get my money back, I need to monetize these views on YouTube Live."

"Ok," said Drew, happy to step back and let Brandon get his hands dirty.

"Hi, viewers! Don't forget to hit subscribe and click that like button!

132

Today, I purchased a box on the DarkWeb from a guy whose screenname was Timmy. I went on 4Chan and had looked around. Apparently, this guy had a ton of five-star reviews for selling other boxes like this one. The other buyers said this guy had dozens of these boxes, that matched up well to real cases. When I contacted 'Timmy,' he directed me to something called 'Tor,' which I used to pay for this box using Bitcoin, an untraceable cryptocurrency. The box arrived today, with no return address. From the postmark, it looks like it was mailed to my house from Baton Rouge, Louisiana on Tuesday, which is odd because it's only Wednesday here in Chicago.

"I just opened it up, and so far, we found this polyester blouse which looks like it is stained with something rusty red, an ice pick and newspaper clippings. There's some other stuff too. I don't know if it's all related, but let's look at them."

Brandon pulled out the first story and held it up to the camera, reading it aloud.

The Daily Chronicle

July 27, 1971

LOCAL AREA WOMAN GOES MISSING

Channel 2 Action News reported yesterday that Marsha Victoria, 23, has been declared missing. Her husband Henry, 24, informed police last Wednesday that she had failed to come home after a routine shopping trip. According to the police report, DeKalb County detectives have been working on her missing person's case but have no leads. Victoria was last seen exiting the Piggly Wiggly in DeKalb, wearing a green blouse and long white skirt. Her car, a blue 1970 Chrysler New Yorker, was found

*abandoned in the store's parking lot. Police ask anyone
with any information to contact them.*

A photograph of a young blonde woman wearing the same top was embedded in the story. Brandon picked up the bloody shirt again and inspected it while the camera continued to record.

"This green blouse has a label on it that says, 'Lord & Taylor', size medium and the little copyright notice is 1970. There are several small holes surrounded by what may be blood. Interesting."

He put the items down and picked up the rusty ice pick, holding it up to the camera. It had a wooden handle that appeared partially stained. A few strands of bloody blonde hair were stuck to it.

"Uh, this is pretty good for a fake. Timmy, the seller, appears to have done a fine job of staging evidence of an old murder. Nicely done. I am particularly impressed that he found a vintage blouse matching the photograph in the news story."

Brandon reached deeper in the box and pulled out several other news clippings, reading them aloud.

The Daily Chronicle

October 19, 1973

*Several months after Marsha Victoria, 23, was reported
missing, her husband Henry has become the prime sus-
pect in her disappearance. DeKalb County detectives
working on the case reported that they received a nearly
anonymous tip from someone calling himself 'Timmy.'
The tipster directed police to a dumpster about a mile
away from where Victoria had gone missing in July. In
the trash, police found compelling physical evidence tying
her husband to the crime. Police did not report publicly*

on the nature of the evidence discovered but commented by saying that it was "unusual" and "potentially incriminating." No body has yet been discovered.

"Ok, so this second story seems to suggest that the husband did it. Or at least that's what police thought back then," said Brandon. "Here's a more recent one," he said, reading aloud.

USA Today

January 9, 1985

The Marsha Victoria case has become one of the most sensational in Georgia history. After reporting her missing in 1971, two years later, Victoria's husband Henry was formally indicted for her murder after police located a note in her husband's own handwriting in a dumpster, seeming to suggest a motive. The note consisted of an explicit threat to his late wife, in which he supposedly told her that he wanted a divorce. He had not previously disclosed this fact to the police. On the note was a bloodstain that matched her blood type.

After an earlier mistrial, a DeKalb jury eventually convicted Henry of second-degree murder based on the circumstantial evidence. Judge Bankman sentenced him to death by lethal injection. After briefly halting the death penalty due to U.S. Supreme Court decisions declaring it unconstitutional, the State of Georgia resumed executions late last year. Henry's appeals having been exhausted, he was executed this New Year's Eve. His body remains unclaimed in the DeKalb County Morgue.

"Ok, so it looks like her husband was executed for her murder a long time ago," said Brandon on camera. "I wonder why this is relevant today."

He then reached into the bottom of the box and found a sealed envelope. The postmark on the envelope was dated July 28, 1971, in Atlanta, Georgia. It appeared to have been mailed from a Post Office Box to the same box.

Brandon held it up to the camera and ripped it open.

"Yesterday afternoon, I drove past the Piggly Wiggly and saw a pretty girl wearing green in the parking lot. It's my favorite color. I followed her with my van. I told her that I needed help getting a flat tire fixed, and when she stood behind the van, I shoved her into the back and gagged and bound her. I drove her about an hour away. I heard her squirming and trying to scream the whole time, but then she got tired and quieted down. I killed her with an ice pick and took my time. I dumped her body where no one will ever find it. When I later went through her purse, I found a handwritten letter from her husband. He was apparently planning on divorcing her. So, I planted his letter with some of her blood in the dumpster and tipped off the police. I hope he fries for it."

"Wow," Brandon said to the camera. "I thought the contents of this box were fake, but it certainly sounds like there could be real evidence of a murder and a frame-up of an innocent man who was executed. I don't know if this is real, but the seller of the box called himself 'Timmy,' and so did the author of the letter in the sealed envelope from 1971. Wait, there's one more envelope that I almost missed."

Brandon reached in and pulled out the final contents of the box. It was another sealed envelope without any postmark on it. He tore it open and read it silently to himself.

"Brandon Figueroa. You paid us five hundred dollars to learn about one of the many, many murders that we have committed over the years. We have framed hundreds of innocent people. Thousands of missing people whose deaths remain unsolved, those are our doing. But perhaps most importantly, we can send boxes of physical evidence to law enforcement agencies around the country to frame you, Brandon, for a dozen unsolved murders. We have already visited your home in Chicago and taken hair samples from your shower drain. We have taken DNA from your toothbrush and lifted fingerprints from all over your possessions. We have your favorite t-shirt and at least twenty-five little pieces of evidence from your closet and bedroom. Your hairs are now embedded on bloody weapons and clothing that can be in the hands of police in several states in a matter of hours. If you assist us with distributing evidence of our past crimes to frame other innocent victims and send us five thousand dollars in Bitcoin, we will never mail any of those other boxes to the police. You know how to contact Timmy. You have twenty-four hours to make your decision. We hope you are smart and join us. We are legion."

Brandon quickly ended the broadcast.

"What does that last letter say?" asked Drew.

"Nothing, it says it was all fake."

"Figures. Good story, though," said Drew. "He really does a convincing job! You should get a lot of views with that one."

"Yeah, good story," said Brandon, sweating. He was frantically thinking about where he could get his hands on five thousand dollars.

ERROR

By Joseph C. Gioconda

I sat in the back row of my AP European History class when I was a high school sophomore in my new town in Kentucky. My blonde girlfriend Tanya sat near me, so we often exchanged little notes to stay awake. My family and I had moved from Cincinnati a year earlier, and Tanya was one of the first girls I met at the bowling alley where I got a job resetting pins. While we argued a lot, we managed to make up afterward with some fun times.

That morning, I was half-asleep listening to my teacher drone on about World War I when two uniformed police officers knocked on our classroom door.

They gestured for my teacher to come outside and talk to them. My classmates and I shot glances at each other. This was the most exciting thing to happen in a while. But then my teacher gestured at me to grab my backpack and come outside. My heart sank, and my mind raced. Did I get caught illegally downloading music? Could they really have caught me doing that?

"Tom, these officers would like a word with you," said my teacher Mr. Grandin.

"Is everything ok?" I asked. I started wondering if my father had gotten into trouble again.

My girlfriend Tanya looked at me with fear in her eyes.

"Just come with us, please," the taller cop said.

I felt my classmates staring at me through the windowpane on the door.

The two police officers led me to the school nurse's office. I had only been in here once when I had a migraine and needed some aspirin and to lay down for a bit.

The cop put on a yellow latex glove and took out a long swab stick and handed me a piece of paper. "Please open your mouth and breathe."

"No! What are you doing?" I asked.

"DNA test," he said. "Here's a search warrant. We already called your parents. They're coming down to meet us. Now, cooperate, and it will be over in a few seconds, ok?"

"What's going on here?" I started to cry a little as he jammed the Q-Tip way up my nose.

"Just open your mouth and breathe, ok?"

I did what he said, listening to his keys and handcuffs jingling on his waist next to his pistol.

I gagged. He put the swab in a plastic tube.

"They should be here soon, so I'll wait to read your rights until then."

"Read my rights? What is going on?"

"I'm not at liberty to say right now. So just hang tight, ok?"

After the longest ten minutes of my life, my father and mother walked into the nurse's office.

"Officers, please step away from him," my father said.

The cops took a single step back but stayed ominously close by.

"What is going on, Mom?" I looked at my mother. I could tell that she had been crying from her red puffy eyes.

"They think you killed that girl," she said, sniffling.

"What girl? What are you talking about?" I asked, almost laughing at the absurdity.

"Just don't say another word," my father told me. "I already called a lawyer. Just sit tight. Officer, can we speak to our son in private, please?"

The officers looked at each other.

"Five minutes, and then we have to bring him down and book him."

They left the room and stood right outside the door.

"Tom, do you remember how they found a body in the river last month?" my father asked me.

"Not really, I don't," I told him truthfully.

"Well, it was all over the news. I guess they did an investigation, and the cops claim that there were skin cells under her fingernails and some hair strands that matched your DNA."

"What," I laughed out loud. "That is freakin' impossible. I never did a thing. What the hell is going on?"

"I know," my father said. "It's ridiculous, but the police came by our house early this morning, and you had already left for school. They told us that they found a 99.99% match with your DNA."

"Wait, how did they have my DNA?"

"Remember when I sent in that kit last year to that company, and they told us that we had some percentage of Native American in us?" my father said.

"Oh yeah, so? That's why they are doing this? That's your DNA, not mine." It seemed laughable.

"Well, we're hopeful that once they have your DNA, they will realize they are making a huge mistake," my mother said.

"99.99%? That means I am obviously in the margin of error or something, right? They catch these mistakes. I mean, they have scientists, right? Doesn't everyone share that same percentage of DNA? Don't they have only your DNA, Dad?"

"I am sure it's all an error," my dad said, looking at my mother nervously. "But they also said our DNA is connected to four other cold cases back in Cincinnati."

GETTYSBURG

By Akilina Popova

"**D**o you smell that?" Tony asked.

"Yeah, it smells like fireworks," William said. "Gunpowder."

"Yeah," said John, pulling over their car to the side of the road and turning off the halogen headlights. "Like that smoky smell after Fourth of July."

The three teenagers got out of the car and stood on the side of the road in Gettysburg. They had decided to take a road trip that summer, and none of them had ever been to the battleground town. They had shared a room at a cheap local motel and drove around during the day to various spots of interest and the visitor's center. There, they heard stories and watched narrated films about the gruesome spectacle that had happened there a century and a half earlier.

In July 1863, they learned a triangle of land where Pickett's Charge happened. It was a bloody scene where an unrelenting artillery bombardment and infantry charges left thousands of men from both sides dead and wounded. Afterward, human carcasses lay for days in the hot July sun.

That first night, the three boys took a drive on the road that winded through the battlefield. Park Rangers didn't want anyone, much less three boys, stomping through the hallowed battlefields at night. But they didn't seem to mind as much if a car driving on the public road pulled over briefly to stare over the wooden fences across the verdant fields.

"I think that smell must be from leftover smoke. Was there a Civil War reenactment that we missed today?" asked John.

"Well, it's after 10. I don't think there were any today, but if there were, they would have been like what, more than 5 hours ago, right?" asked Tony.

"Wait, what the hell is that?" John asked, pointing across the field to the north. "Look!"

A wisp of bluish vapor drifted slowly like a patch of smoke.

"I think it's just fog," Tony said.

"But it's luminescent," William said.

"Yeah," said John. "It's glowing, and there's no moon." He stopped in silence. "Look at it more closely. Am I losing it?"

All three squinted to peer across the football field-sized land between them and the bluish vapors. The night was dark, and they had turned off the headlights, so their eyes were still adjusting. The smell of used gunpowder was only getting stronger.

"Soldiers marching," Tony said.

"Oh my God, I see it too," said William. "And they're coming this way."

OFFICE

By Joseph C. Gioconda

T welve years ago, I rented a small office in a building that was a factory built about nearly two centuries ago. And it has the scars to prove it.

Originally, a Hosiery Mill operated out of this building. In 1872, the Excelsior Bobbin and Spool Works was founded by John R. Lawson. In 1892, it was moved to a nearby town after a fire destroyed the original plant. In 1902, the Bobbin and Spool Works chartered the name Excelsior Bobbin and Spool Company, which expanded with new buildings and updated equipment. After the brief tenure of the stocking manufacturer, the building was used by a stained-glass company, a bobbin factory, and then, during World War II, by the LaRoche Aircraft Corporation.

When World War II started, there was a tremendous demand for aircraft, and LaRoche expanded to meet the demand. To mark its success, a ceremony was held at the plant in July 1945, where the company was awarded the Army-Navy "E" for excellence in production. After the war, the company changed over to stainless steel production for jet engines, missiles, and satellites. The world's first weather satellite was manufactured here. It recorded the first TV image from space. Some of the components used in the Apollo space missions were also manufactured here. In recent years, the property has been renovated into office space.

There were many typical factory accidents and fires over the two centuries the building has stood. It was widely reported that in the mid-1800s, a worker for Excelsior had gotten caught between a spooling machine and a brick wall. The antiquated machine had come loose from its moorings and a wire wrapped around the man's waist. He was disemboweled in a matter of seconds.

Another documented story involved the time in the 1950s when the building was used to assemble jet engines by LaRoche. A woman had gotten her arm stuck in a fan blade which pulled her entire body into the machine, severing her carotid artery. She died quickly and messily as her blood spurted all over the walls.

Another story involves a fire that took place during the era when the building was used for stained glass. At least four women died.

My own secluded office space in the old factory has 25-foot ceilings and all the original stained brick walls, as well as exposed pipes and heating ducts. During the day, the office is well-lit and perfectly pleasant, although clearly very old.

At night, however, it suddenly feels palpably different. I always feel like someone is watching me from above, hovering over me from afar. My secretary refuses to work a minute after dark, even for double overtime pay.

Just last week, I was getting a haircut at a barbershop a few blocks from my office. The barber asked me where I work, so I told him.

He asked, "You mean the haunted factory?"

"What do you mean?" I asked.

He said, "Well, I have several friends that have worked in there over the years, as real estate lawyers and finance guys. None of them will work there alone. They hear screams and blood-curdling noises. One guy said that he sees and hears shadows moving and talking to each other all the time. He heard laughing and screams."

"Seriously?" I asked.

"Yes, my friends want nothing to do with that place after dark. Especially not after the recent suicide."

I paused and asked, "Suicide? What are you talking about?"

He said, "Not long ago, the janitor was having marital problems and hanged himself from the pipe in the rafters. The story didn't make the news because the new building owners didn't want bad PR to hurt their rent if tenants freaked out."

The crazy thing is that I remember this maintenance worker.

When I told my wife this story, she stopped abruptly and said, "What did he look like? The guy?"

I said, "Well, if I recall, he was in his early 60's and had thin gray hair."

She said, "Oh my God, I think I saw his ghost. Last month, I went into your building and used the restroom in the basement. I distinctly remember seeing him coming out of the women's restroom, which startled me. I said to him, 'Oh, sorry! I didn't know you were in there' and the odd thing was that he walked by me as if I didn't exist. He didn't look at me or say a word. Then, when I turned around, he was gone. Just gone, as though he was never there. I figured I must have missed seeing him go into some hidden doorway, but I distinctly remember being really confused at the time."

I should mention that my wife is a very rational, well-educated skeptic.

Tonight, I was working alone after hours, and I was using video recording software to capture some narration for a presentation.

When I played it back, I heard a clear, crisp voice say, "Go home to your pretty wife."

BLINDMAN

By Grace Elizabeth

"What do you mean you aren't coming?" Mary practically screamed down the phone at Jemima.

Spencer giggled as he watched his lover pace around the room impatiently. Mary huffed loudly and pressed the bright red speaker button so Spencer could listen in.

"You have heard the rumours, just as me and Darrel! I won't endanger my life or my brothers."

Spencer laughed obnoxiously and made his way over to the phone.

"Don't be ridiculous; those rumours are superstition—only a fool would take them seriously." He could practically feel Jemima rolling her eyes over the phone.

"We aren't coming, end of story."

A loud beep sounded, and Mary fell on the bed and let out a feral grunting noise.

"The rumours aren't even true!" she yelled.

Spencer sat down beside her and put a hand on her knee.

"I don't even remember the whole story of Blind Man's Bluff! So, it can't be that awful," she said.

Spencer sighed and began to retell the infamous story that had been told in their quaint town for decades.

"Legend says that a crazed man lived in the cabin in solitude—when he got tired of living on his own, he gouged his eyes out and died from blood loss."

The look of pure disgust on Mary's face made Spencer snort.

"But we will be fine, don't panic!"

Mary pushed herself off the bed and grabbed Spencer's hand. She pulled him out the door, and they began their journey towards the cabin in the woods, the cabin named *Bindman's Bluff.*

A few hours later, after practically ruining their voice boxes by screaming at the top of their lungs to whatever song from a radio signal they could get, they arrived at the cabin in North Idaho. A red truck was parked outside the garage, so they figured that Poppy, Emma, and Toby must have already arrived. A small, blonde bundle of joy leapt from the doorway—it was Emma. She rushed to Mary's car door and practically ripped it open; her face lit up as Mary hugged her tightly.

"Where on earth have you been? Night has almost fallen!" A look of dismay clouded the girl's joyful features. "Where are Jemima and Darrel?" Mary held her hand tightly as Spencer got out of the car to greet Poppy and Toby.

"They got scared by the rumours about this place; they can't be true—"

Toby interrupted her.

"Well, Mary, we'll be finding out today as we are playing the Blindman's Bluff tonight!"

"What on earth do you mean?" Mary giggled.

Poppy came around the corner, her black afro drawing all the attention as usual.

"One of us wears a blindfold, and the others move around the room. If the blindfolded person captures someone, they take their place as the Blindman."

Mary nodded, looking skeptical.

"But," Poppy said, "the rumours are that if you play the game between one and three in the morning, the Blindman will rise from the dead and kill you all!"

Spencer rolled his eyes at her exaggerated tones.

"Wait, where is Archie?" Mary asked.

"He had to stay late at work, but he will be here soon," replied Poppy.

Toby pulled three bottles of vodka from his trunk, and Poppy flashed a couple of bags of pot and winked. Emma yelled for help as she dragged their suitcases inside on her own. All five friends followed Emma into the dreary cabin and got ready to play the game.

"So, I just put the blindfold on and then try and find you all?" Emmy asked.

Poppy nodded, and Spencer helped her tie the blindfold around her eyes. Her eyes were burning slightly... it was probably from the amount of pot they had smoked.

"What's the time?" she asked, knowing full well her voice was becoming slurred from the alcohol.

"It is..." Toby checked his phone "one o'clock, perfect! So, who's ready to get brutally murdered by the Blindman?"

Mary heard a whack as Poppy smacked Toby over the head.

"Shut up; you are so annoying." Mary stood up, trying to catch her balance with what limited sight she had. She could hear the pitter-patter of her friend's feet as they ran around the large living room.

Mary started walking. Hearing her friends giggle quietly as she got closer, she reached out in front of her and skimmed someone's skin. But they ran.

"Dammit! This is so hard," Mary complained, laughing as she became disoriented. The taste of alcohol didn't help. A small buzzing sound came from above her as the lights flickered slightly.

"That was spooky," whispered Emma.

"Oh please, it's an old house in the middle of nowhere; the electrics aren't going to be great, are they?" Spencer said, receiving a loud hushing sound from Poppy.

Mary heard a loud crash and some chuckling as one of her friends fell into the table. Mary kept stumbling around, bumping into random bits of furniture, her blindfold seemed to be becoming increasingly tighter, her mind becoming more and more clouded as the seconds ticked by.

"Guys, that's not funny!" Poppy shouted.

"What?" Toby asked, a hint of amusement in his tone.

"Turn the lights back on!" The room was silent. "Guys, seriously, this isn't funny."

Mary stopped moving.

"Poppy, the lights are on…" Emma mumbled, her words slurred and hard to understand.

"Okay, guys, I am getting seriously creeped out," Mary said. "Let's take a break." She tugged at the blindfold, but it didn't move. "What the…"

Mary pulled harder, the blindfold getting tighter with each tug. Toby screamed as something smashed to the floor, and everything went black.

"Nobody moves!" Mary shouted. "I can't get my blindfold off, Spence can you help me?" Mary felt him tug at the back of her blindfold, but he was making it tighter. "Stop! Spence, what are you doing?" She heard Emma let out a quiet cry.

"Mary," Spencer said… but that couldn't be right; his voice was coming from the other side of the room. "Nobody has moved."

Mary lept away from whatever the hell was touching her blindfold. She didn't get a chance to calm her breathing before Toby started screaming, his speech was incomprehensible.

"Toby!" Spencer screamed as Poppy and Emma ran to where his voice was coming from. There was a thud, and suddenly Toby went silent.

"Can anyone see anything?" Mary asked, her voice cracking. She could feel the tears forming in her eyes, but they were kept stationary by her painfully tight blindfold. Nobody said anything; the only sounds were the deep breaths taken by her and her friends.

"No," Poppy whispered, "No, we can't."

Emma's breathing was becoming heavier and heavier; her palms were becoming sweaty. Then the screaming started once again. Emma's shrieks were hoarse and shrill; they were blood halting.

"Dear God!" Mary shouted as she started to panic. Her eyes became sore and stuffy as the tears plagued them. Then she started moving, it was a foolish choice, but she had panicked. She tripped, letting out a yelp as she grabbed someone. Their skin was cold; a chill ran down her spine. "Who—" she breathed. "Who is this?"

Poppy cried from the corner; it wasn't her. Spencer breathed from beside her; it wasn't him... *so who was it?* Mary felt a freezing breeze brush through her hair, and she stumbled backwards over what had to be one of her friends' bodies. She felt her heart drop as her hands landed in something warm and sticky; she couldn't stop herself screaming as she scrambled backwards to where she had heard Spencer. She felt two reassuring hands hold her shoulders as he tried to calm her down.

"I'm going to try and find the door," said Emma, her voice was raspy and broken, and a few stray sniffles broke her brave façade.

Mary listened for the thud of Emma's feet as she made her way to the door. She had barely taken a few steps before she started gasping. A gurgling sound broke from her throat, and she started screaming.

"My eyes! My eyes!!" She exclaimed, "God, make it stop! Please, God, make it..."

Everything went silent, until the sound of a body hitting the floor echoed throughout the room yet again.

Mary cried out, her body shaking with fear; Spencer whispered gently in her ear. He was still trying to calm her, but it wasn't working. Nothing would calm her shaking nerves. Her sobbing was too loud for her to realise that Spencer's breath had become hoarse.

"No, please…" Mary whimpered as Spencer's screams pierced her very soul. She wished, she prayed that this thing would kill her, that she didn't have to hear her lover die. A loud thud sent her heart to her stomach. Suddenly her blindfold became loose, and she tugged it downwards hesitantly. She couldn't stop the ear-piercing screech that left her body at what she saw.

Archie waltzed towards the door; it was eerily quiet. He expected his friends to still be awake; it had barely struck two o'clock. He reached for the door handle but paused as he saw the door was not only unlocked but slightly ajar. Strange. Surely his friends wouldn't be stupid enough to leave the door unlocked, not at this time of night anyway—they were dumb but didn't lack common sense.

"Hello."

It was more of a question than a statement. The room was completely dark, but a low sniffling noise came from the corner. He switched the light on and became faint at the sight; his heart dropped to the bottom of his stomach. His breath completely hitched. His friends were scattered on the floor, pools of blood encircled their heads. And their eyes… their eyes were hollow holes as if they had been gouged out. He dropped his bags, and his eyes slowly moved to the corner where Mary was sitting. Her eyes were open but bloody; blood stained her cheeks as if hellish tears had fallen from her eyes. Her stare was vacant, as if nothing were in her soul or mind.

"Blindman's Bluff, Blindman's Bluff…" She repeated these words over and over.

And as Archie stared at his friends, he could have sworn, out of the corner of his eye, he saw an old man with no eyes smiling back at him.

31

PARTY

By Joseph C. Gioconda

Every year, it seemed like Jake's Halloween parties got wilder. He wasn't a particularly good-looking guy, but he had a knack for socializing with all the people who you'd want at the perfect party. He hung around the local pubs and befriended the most popular bartenders and waitresses. He made friends with the college-age girls who worked at the local nail salons. They all made the perfect costume party guests.

Since he was still single and in his early thirties without any student loan debt, he could afford to build and construct a dazzling house for himself. He made a very lucrative living as a union construction foreman. Many of the mothers in town repeated to their daughters that Jake was a good catch. He never disputed their characterization but was having too much fun to consider settling down just yet. In the meantime, planning his annual Halloween party occupied his thoughts and finances for several months during and after the summer. It even took him weeks to clean up afterward. It was becoming an annual tradition in town.

Jake's house couldn't handle more than twenty or thirty people comfortably, but he nonetheless regularly invited over ninety, and sometimes a hundred and twenty showed up. The front lawn, yard, and even the streets in front of his house were transformed into a rager every October 31. His neighbors didn't like it, but they tolerated it once a year as Jake was otherwise a friendly and accommodating neighbor who did odd construction projects for them for free. A few neighbors even showed up to the festivities from time to time.

Past guests started telling their friends about this annual party and invited their friends. It had gotten so crazy that he had to hire an off-duty cop as a bouncer and bring in professional bartenders to card people crashing the party because many were underage kids looking for free drinks.

Nonetheless, this year, Jake wanted to outdo himself. He searched on Craigslist for psychic mediums who worked private parties. His idea was to have a woman dressed like a gypsy come in and read people's fortunes. He figured he could pay her a hundred bucks and have her read palms and tarot cards all night. Such atmospherics only added to the charm. He already had enough decorations and animatronics to outfit the entire house and yard, but having a real live psychic would be a great new addition to the mystical décor.

When it turned midnight on Halloween, Jake's party was raging. Pop music blared from a pre-recorded playlist on the iPod through a party speaker with a spinning disco ball on top. However, the instant the middle-aged woman and her entourage walked in the front door, the air got colder, darker.

In an e-mail, Jake had specifically requested that the woman wear stereotypical gypsy attire: a kerchief and a flowing colorful dress. Instead, she was short, completely pale, had a short black bob haircut, and wore a large black sweatshirt and yoga pants. She looked nothing like a traditional fortune teller, yet simultaneously looked nothing like a normal person. She had pale blue eyes that pierced right through him.

Jake noticed that some guests appeared to have left the party abruptly, and the rooms were starting to clear out. The dance music had also been turned down, although he hadn't seen anyone go near the iPod or speaker.

"You must be… Jacob," she said, extending her hand. "I am Vadoma."

"Jake, you can call me Jake," he said.

"I only use full birth names to avoid confusing the spirits," she said, her eyes darting around the room. "Is this where we will hold my séance?"

"I thought you were just doing readings."

"I am. But the spirits will not talk to me unless I call upon them first. And that takes a specific ritual. Please meet my sons Danior and Bartley. They will be assisting."

Two hulking men stood nearby in a menacing manner. One of them put down a large old stereo boombox that looked thirty years old onto the floor.

"Nice to meet you," Jake said. "Ok, so let's get you started. What do you need, Vadoma?"

"Chairs. Everyone must sit and be silent. Oh, and a small table for an altar," she said.

"Altar? Um, I'm not sure—"

"—We just call it that," Danior interrupted Jake. "A formality."

"Ok, I think you can use this card table. What else?" Jake asked.

"I brought my own supplies," said the woman, pulling black candles and a handful of bones out of a plastic supermarket shopping bag and setting them on the table in the shape of an X.

Jake couldn't tell if they were animal or human bones.

"Gather everyone, and please turn all the lights and music down," she said, lighting black candles on either side of the table.

"Uh, everyone, our fortune teller is starting a ritual. Please come in and sit down," Jake announced.

"Ritual?" said a thin blonde girl who was dressed in a skimpy mermaid costume that bared her tight midriff. "I'm out of here," she said, grabbing her purse and walking straight out the front door.

"No way, I'm staying, I gotta see this," said a tipsy brunette dressed as a sexy cowgirl, sitting down drunkenly gripping a red plastic cup in her hand.

A dozen party guests stood and sat around Vadoma, giggling and chuckling at the spectacle.

Danior hit play on the tape deck. Rhythmic drums started to play in the background.

"Good evening, spirits!" shouted Vadoma dramatically. "Greetings from our world to yours. I call upon you in the house of Jacob to be present and show yourselves tonight, on the feast of Samhain. We call upon you to break through the veils of the worlds that separate us."

The drums continued and intensified.

"I call upon the shades of the dead by Abdia, Orelno, Abrasax, and Abreu!"

"What the hell is going on in here?" asked a male drunken party guest dressed as a superhero, stumbling into the room, and spilling his drink.

"Shh, it's a ritual," said the drunk cowgirl.

"A what?" laughed the superhero. "Get the hell outta here, put the freakin' music back on!" he shouted, hitting play on the iPod.

"Silence!" screamed Vadoma. "I said, turn that off!"

Just as she said so, the electricity in the house flickered, and the lights completely went out. Her tape deck, powered by battery, continued to play the drumbeat even louder, it seemed.

"Whoa, did you do that, gypsy lady?" asked the superhero.

"You have offended me and the spirits by your insolence," said Vadoma. "Apologize to Eddie."

"Who the hell is Eddie?" laughed the drunk cowgirl.

"My dead son," Vadoma whispered.

"Ok, this is getting just a little creepy," said the cowgirl.

"I agree," said Jake, stepping forward from the group. "Vadoma, can we talk for a minute?"

The woman's eyes started to roll back in her head, so only the whites were visible. She started to make a guttural sound. "Eddie....Eddie," she muttered in a hoarse voice.

"Mom are you ok?" asked Bartley, shooting a glance at his brother Danior.

"You mean this isn't part of her act?" asked Jake.

"No," said Danior. "This never happened before."

The cowgirl started to quiver in the metal folding chair. She dropped her red plastic cup, and alcohol spilled all over the carpet. Her eyes rolled back in her head, too, so she resembled Vadoma, who was standing across the room, facing her.

"Momma!" the cowgirl yelled in a young boy's voice, standing up. "It's me, Eddie. I'm back."

MOTHER

By Joseph C. Gioconda

"You designed a weapon of mass destruction?"

"No. As international law defines it, a weapon of mass destruction is a nuclear, radiological, chemical, biological, or other device that is intended to harm a large number of people. This is a weapon, but it kills only one person. It's even more precise than a drone strike, which could accidentally kill a bystander. No, this is the most advanced, efficient one mankind has ever created. Safer than an assassination. No standing federal law criminalizes the assassination of a foreign official outside the boundaries of the United States, you know."

"I see," said the young new scientist who had recently joined the program.

The two men stood inside a highly secure facility inside a mountain in remote Colorado, fourteen stories underground. The hum of the fluorescent lights were the only sounds audible in the lab.

"I've been working down here for a long, long time. Can't say I see sunlight much anymore. But that's ok. My mother invented someone called the heart attack gun, have you heard of it?"

"No, I haven't," said the new scientist.

"In the sixties, they needed a weapon to take care of the targets on the CIA blacklist without leaving any trace that would bring up suspicions in the media. One of the hot targets was Castro. Killing people from a distance was the go-to choice, but every bullet can be traced back. Getting too close to the target would risk the agent being compromised."

"Right," said the new scientist.

"My mother was the first Nobel award-winning scientist to work for the CIA. I basically grew up down here, except when I went to school to get my degrees. My mother came up with a gun that would shoot poisoned projectiles that would dissolve inside the target and induce a heart attack which would be undetectable upon post-mortem. Animals, as well as prisoners, were used to test the weapon. It worked."

"Was it ever used to assassinate anyone?"

"Can't say," the older scientist smiled. "The gun had the ability to shoot the poisoned projectile from 100 meters with good accuracy. It had a pretty good range and scope.

The real problem was that it leaked. Too many idiots within the agency promoted it, so the media found out about it as using some sort of 'death ray' to provoke a cardiac attack onto its victims, making it sound as if it was out of a science fiction movie.

"Back then, the Church Committee was jumping on every piece of evidence that was coming out about the CIA. In '75, people wanted to know more about what the CIA was doing. Gerald Ford was forced to ban any tactics of targeted assassination conducted by the CIA and any other intelligence agencies. For us, this was a massive blow as most of the information from this event had leaked to the KGB, showing not only the capabilities we had.

"After my Mom passed away, I got her notes. She had an idea that I perfected. I continued her legacy," he smiled.

"And what was that?"

The older scientist flipped over a white board on an easel. "Let me show you."

He drew on the board a double helix that he had become accustomed to depicting over the many years as the CIA's leading scientist.

"Human DNA is 99.9% identical from person to person, and although 0.1% difference doesn't sound like a lot, it actually represents millions of different locations within the genome where variation can occur, equating to a breathtakingly large number of potentially unique DNA sequences.

"So, each human has billions of possible base pairs for each of these chromosomes. Therefore, we are essentially unique. Even twins have different DNA, albeit only very slightly different."

"I know all that. So how does that idea work as a weapon?" asked the new scientist.

"I took the generic flu virus and made it dormant. It's the same flu virus that has been around for millions of years. Everyone on the planet already has immunity from it, either from having contracted it before or from a flu vaccine. In any event, it's no more virulent than the flu vaccine itself. Somebody might get a sniffle, but that's it. Completely harmless, in fact."

"Ok."

"But I added one big difference. A protein spike that can only enter one person's cells: Our target. I get a sample of his DNA from a spy. Usually a strand of hair or skin cells. Not hard to get. I tweak the virus to only infect that DNA strand. Then our spies release it into his environment.

"Can be released anywhere, but let's assume we release it in the country, city, or town where our target is likely to be located. It will then spread through the general population. Its function has been improved in our lab, so it is highly contagious, each person infecting up to a hundred more people within a day or two. It is airborne, you see."

"Scary," said the new scientist.

"It will infect a small city in a matter of a week, maybe two, depending on the weather. It quickly reaches our target. Within a day, he is infected and dies from a sudden heart attack. There is no way to trace the cause of his myocardial infarction back to my virus. It looks like his ticker just gave out. In the United States alone, someone has a heart attack every forty seconds. Number one killer. No one suspects foul play, and even if they do, they can't prove it.

"But the virus was actually programmed to attack and destroy heart muscle—and only the target's heart muscle. Out of eight billion people on earth, only one heart will stop. Once the target dies, the virus dies out. It only has a life expectancy of a few months. It is programmed to mutate to a new strain that self-destructs."

"Wow, that is brilliant, I must admit. But there must be some danger to it, no? What if it mutates into another new strain? One that you didn't expect."

"Impossible. I put another protein spike on it that renders it not only otherwise harmless, but it will eventually infect and destroy itself. There won't be a single strand of this virus left on the planet in a few months, except in this test tube. But if the media finds out about it, we couldn't use it anymore."

"Has it been used? To assassinate anyone?"

The scientist smiled.

"Mother would be proud."

33

GASLIGHTING

By Joseph C. Gioconda

"**D**o you know what that book's about?" the middle-aged man asked June.

"Not really," the girl said. "It's in a section of your store called 'Revenge Books,' so that interested me."

"It's about ruining someone's life. Not in a funny way, either. Like driving them to the brink of madness. I don't recommend using that book lightly," he said while stroking a black cat that had curled up on his lap. Several other cats slinked nearby, jealous of his attention.

The man sat behind the counter at the used bookstore in downtown New York City. The little shop on St. Mark's Place in Greenwich Village seemed to stock edgy books, not the kind you'd find at Barnes & Noble. Sections included 'Anarchy,' 'Identity Theft,' 'How to Hack Computers,' 'Hiding Bodies,' and worse.

"Well, after last weekend, I might need it," she said.

"Someone break your heart?" he asked.

"More than you know," she muttered.

"Well, it's not a very long book, what is it, around a hundred pages?" he asked.

She flipped to the end. "Ninety-nine."

"But it's so good; it doesn't have to be very long. If you follow the detailed instructions to the letter, you won't even need to get to the end. Your enemy will be destroyed by page sixty-six, I predict. At least, that's what I've been told. But revenge is some serious business, young lady. You should never serve it up unless you are ready to reap what you sow."

"I'll take it," she said, putting it down on the counter. "How much?"

"Twenty dollars."

"Expensive," she said.

"Worth every penny, if you know what I mean," he smirked, putting the bill into the cash register. "Let's put it in a brown paper bag," he said. "Don't get caught reading it, and don't tell anyone where you got it. If you want, when you're done using it, come back here, and I'll buy it back from you. I've re-sold that same copy ten times already."

"Um, ok," she said, walking out the front door with her newfound treasure.

The man shook his head. "She'll be back in a month, Bastet," he whispered to the cat. "You'll see..."

Holding the tattered book in hand, June walked down the busy Manhattan Street toward her favorite coffee shop on the corner. She went in and sat down, ordered a double espresso, and got to work reading.

The first chapter introduced the term gaslighting. Apparently, there was a dramatic 1944 movie starring Ingrid Bergman that led to the use of the term to describe an elaborate plot to psychologically wear someone down to achieve their complete destruction. In the film, the husband periodically dims the gas lamps. His wife repeatedly asks her husband to confirm her perceptions about the dimming lights, and he repeatedly insists the lights have not changed. His intention is to disrupt her mentally so that he can justify commitment to a mental institution.

June's relationship with Shane had always been fraught. From the minute that she first met him at a bar in SoHo, she suspected he would be trouble. She had asked him why he had a tan line on his left ring finger, and he came up with some explanation she knew wasn't true. She figured he was married and cheating but let that slide. This was New York City, after all. At least she let it slide until she discovered his wife was pregnant.

Yet, she still couldn't break it off with him. They had so much fun together; she just couldn't bring herself to tell him to take a hike. So, instead, they spent every weekend holed up in her apartment. They had their fun, ordered Chinese food, and he told his wife that he was traveling for work a lot.

Finally, June's friend Natalie invited her to a birthday party at the same bar where she had met Shane on a weeknight. When she saw him in the corner making out with another girl, she couldn't believe it. Not only was he cheating on his wife, but he was also cheating on June. That was the last straw.

June thought about contacting Shane's wife and destroying his marriage by telling her everything. But that would be too easy. Now that she had this book, she could explore more creative opportunities to right his wrongs.

June carefully read Chapter 1. She paid for her espresso and walked down Second Avenue to a convenience store where she stocked up on pre-paid gift cards and calling cards that she purchased with a few hundred dollars in cash she had withdrawn from an ATM. In Chapter 1, the book had explained that the use of throwaway burner cards would allow her to make all types of purchases and calls that were essentially untraceable.

When she got home, she used the cards to call several florists in the area. She arranged to have a small bouquet of flowers sent to Shane's office every single day for a week. The card with each said, "Congratulations! From All Your Female Admirers."

The purpose of this exercise, the book said, was to begin to arouse suspicions at his workplace. As a corporate lawyer, Shane's apparent indiscretions would not go unnoticed by his partners and clients, and certainly not his secretary or paralegal.

The next day, June read Chapter 2. Before work, she put on a revealing black dress and a blonde wig to cover her red hair. She added a hefty dose of perfume, put on excessive makeup, and took a cab to Shane's office before he arrived.

She asked for him by name at the building's lobby front desk. When the security guard dialed upstairs, she said she was angry that he hadn't called her and that she wanted to leave him a message to call her. She wrote down a fake number and gave it to the security guard. The number was Shane's own home phone number. The message dispatched to Shane from the building was that an angry blonde girl with streaked makeup had been visiting downstairs and left a number. He'd see the number was his own home.

Chapter 3 instructed June to go to Shane's home, which was located half an hour away. She took a cab, paid with cash, and left a mysterious note on his car windshield in lipstick. It simply said, "Love." She giggled when she thought about how he would explain that one to his wife.

Chapter 4 explained that next, rather than alienate Shane, she should do quite the opposite. She called him and asked if he wanted to get together again at her apartment this weekend. When he arrived that night, he was a mess.

"Jane, are you screwing with me?" he asked her angrily.

"What? What the hell are you talking about?" she asked.

He then recounted to her all the various acts that had been perpetrated on him recently by an unknown stalker.

"Oh my God, Shane," she said. "You really need to get to the bottom of this," she declared, offering her complete assistance. "Who could be doing such a thing to you? This is serious. This woman went to your office and house? Have you called the police?"

"No," he said, sweating. "I need it to stop. But if I call the police, all hell will break loose."

"Please let me help you. I love you; I hate seeing you like this. So, let's figure this out together. What do you know about a psycho who would do this stuff to you?"

"Not much; the security guard downstairs at my building said she was a blonde and smelled like cheap perfume."

"That's crazy," she said. "Do you know anyone like that?"

"No," he said. "That's what has me wracking my brain."

"Could it be your wife?" she asked.

"What? No, why would you suggest that?"

"Could it be that your wife knows about us and is torturing you?"

"God, I never thought of that. But she's not blonde."

"Hmm, couldn't be her then," she mused.

That night, after he fell asleep, June got into his iPhone and copied the passwords from his work e-mail. She also wrote down some of his frequently dialed telephone numbers and rearranged them.

On Monday, he arrived at work. No more flowers had been delivered, so he felt relieved. However, he had several strange voicemail messages waiting for him.

"Shane, this is Paul. Look, I know we've had our disagreements in the past, but I really do appreciate the kind offer. Sure, if you want to buy me tickets to the Superbowl, that would be awesome!"

Paul had been a former client of Shane's at the law firm who had parted ways on less-than-ideal terms. Shane had no idea why he would be under the impression that Paul would offer him expensive sporting event tickets. But now, he couldn't withdraw the misunderstanding. He was stuck buying the tickets.

On Tuesday, Shane got an even stranger message left with his secretary.

"Mr. Tryllis?"

"Yes, Suzy?"

"Your doctor called."

"My doctor?"

"Yes, she told me to tell you that the STD test was negative and that there's nothing to worry about."

"Um, what?"

"She didn't leave a name, but I wrote down the Caller ID. Do you want it?"

"Yes, please, thank you. What did her voice sound like?"

"Authoritative, like a doctor, I don't really know. I didn't recognize it."

Shane took the post-it note from his secretary and dialed it. The number was non-functioning.

He picked up his phone and tried to dial June by clicking on her name to ask for her guidance. The phone rang.

"Hi, June, it's me."

"Shane?"

"Um, hello?"

"Shane, it's your wife. Who did you think you were calling?"

"Um, no one. I mean, you. I knew I was calling you."

"Shane, who is June?"

"Who?"

"You said 'June, it's me.'"

"No, I didn't. I said 'hi, honey, it's me….'"

His wife hung up the phone.

June met Shane at the bar the following weekend. He was becoming disheveled and was already waiting for her with three empty martini glasses when she arrived.

"June bug, I'm glad to see you," he slurred.

"You look like shit, Shane. What's going on?"

"My life is over, that's what's going on," he said, staring down into his fourth drink.

"What do you mean?"

"Well, my firm claims that there were e-mails that had been sent from my account to clients, accusing my partners of defrauding and overbilling them. When I looked, there were no such e-mails in my sent box, so I have no idea what they are talking about. But they let me go."

"Oh my God, Shane," she said, covering her mouth.

"Then, I started getting envelopes in the mail with threats in them. No return address. Bizarre."

"What the hell?"

"My wife is leaving me, too. She suspects... us."

"Oh no, Shane, that is just terrible," she said. "How did she find out?"

"I really don't know, she won't tell me, but you don't have to worry. I covered for you. She doesn't know anything about you."

June bristled and thought about coming clean. She thought about telling him off. She thought about admitting that she had sent out his work e-mails from an Internet café and sent him the death threats through the mail, but that was illegal and might even get him his job back. So, she stayed silent.

"June, I just want us to be together."

"Hah!" she laughed out loud. "So let me get this right. You lost your job, your wife left you and will probably bankrupt you in alimony and child support, you're facing a homicide investigation, and now, you want us to stay together?"

"Investigation? What are you talking about?" He looked up from his drink.

"Oh, you didn't hear? I was watching a show about some unsolved crimes, and I reached out to the police. Turns out you had a lot more in common with some of these wackos out there. A homeless guy was murdered a few blocks from here last month. Was so tragic. The weird thing is that I recognized the murder weapon when I saw it in the news.

It was part of the tool kit that I had gotten you for Christmas last year. When I showed the police the kit, and they took fingerprints, well, let's just say they will have some questions for you."

"Here's your twenty dollars back, young lady," the store owner said, handing the money to June.

"You were right; I only got to page 62, didn't even need to get to the end," she said, handing him back the tattered book.

"Yeah, like I said, the last few chapters aren't really necessary. Once you get to the murder frameups, you are pretty much near the end of the line."

"Did anyone ever get to the end of the book, that you know of?"

"Possibly," he smiled.

Suddenly, three New York City Police officers rushed into the store, and grabbed June by the wrists and handcuffed her.

"That's her, officers," said the shop owner. "She murdered the homeless man and set up her boyfriend. Sent him death threats through the mail, hacked his e-mails, everything's in there."

"What?!" she screamed as they dragged her into the back of the waiting police cruiser.

"Here's the roadmap to convicting her, Officers," he said, handing the book to the arresting officer. "But after the trial, can I have it back? I only have a few copies left, and I like to keep them circulating. Keeps the riffraff off the streets, you know?"

He stroked his black cat.

"One month, Bastet, isn't that what I predicted?"

The cat purred and put its head back down.

"They never read to the end of the book."

Made in United States
Orlando, FL
21 April 2022

17070405R00104